I0760547

MANY ARE INVITED

A NOVEL

DENNIS CUESTA

celestial eyes press

CELESTIAL EYES PRESS

This is a work of fiction. Names, characters, places, and incidents are either a product of the author's imagination or used fictitiously. Locales and public names are sometimes used for atmospheric purposes. Any resemblance to actual people, living or dead, or to businesses, companies, events, institutions, or locales is entirely coincidental.

Published by Celestial Eyes Press, San Jose, California

www.celestialeyespress.com

Library of Congress Control Number: 2022903516
LC record available at https://lccn.loc.gov/2022903516

Many Are Invited/ Dennis Cuesta

ISBN 978-1-957885-00-1

To Jamie

For many are invited, but few are chosen.

Matthew 22:14

Goertz Housewarming

Saturday, 12/18/99, at 6:00 p.m.

316 Mistral Ave, Los Gatos

Drinks, Hors d'oeuvres, Desserts

No Gifts!

The invitation remained hidden in nineteenth-century Russia for over twenty years. I must have been reading *The Brothers Karamazov* when I received the invitation, got some ways into the novel—page 52, apparently—and never picked the book back up again. Maybe because I was only a tenth of the way through and knew the futility of ever trying to finish it—like my dad's 1970 'Cuda, still on blocks the day he died. Or maybe it was a subconscious decision, avoiding anything that would remind me of that evening in 1999.

Tragedy yearns to be mourned and remembered and mourned some more. And in the weeks that followed December 18, I performed that tribute, replaying the events in my head. I ate or walked or showered, and my mind tranced to that crisp night. And not just the horrific end. I'd relive the entire night as if I were watching a film. And though it would always end with the same result—death—the fault might vary. Who was really to blame?

Instead of dissipating over a few weeks, the guilt and grief burrowed deeper inside of me. It eventually became a debilitating burden, and I began to drink to forget that night—or to be more precise, I would drink to blunt my emotions enough to fall asleep. Fearing myself, living a restless mixture of alcoholism, despondency, and disappointment, I sought out help.

Reverend Father Michael Papoutsis headed the Greek Orthodox church that I attended. I had barely ever met the man since I went to church twice a year, and confession wasn't something I had done since coming out to the West Coast. Nevertheless, Father Michael, wearing his vestments, warmly greeted me in the lobby of the church. I followed him into the sanctuary down the main aisle. Near the front, just past the blue and white Greek flag, were two chairs that faced each other. The priest sat down with his back to the wall, an icon of St. Alexis above him. After a short prayer and having laid his white and gold stole over me, Father Michael instructed me to begin. Thirty seconds into it, he raised his hand to me. "No need for details. Know that the Lord already knows your heart. Besides, I'm a little busy today. I need to finalize some things for our annual festival." Without the particulars, my confession would have sounded absurdly overdramatic. My eyes lifted to St. Alexis, and I mumbled something about a mistake back in December before being handed a card. I read aloud a prayer, and even though the priest reassured me in his soft, soothing voice that all was forgiven, the burden did not diminish.

A few days later I made an appointment to see a shrink—well, technically not a shrink. A therapist. Never in my life before this did I think I'd ever seek counseling. Therapists were for other people. But I had unquestionably lost control of my life. I was desperate.

The first session with Melinda P. Omene, LPC, LMFT, didn't go at all as planned. It was a half-hour session, and I needed every minute to explain what had happened that night. Skipping to the end would have been like lobbing a dud grenade, and she might have diagnosed me as mad. So when *Mel*, as she preferred to be called, started asking me about my background and hobbies and interests as if we were on a blind date, I knew there wasn't going to be enough time to tell my story properly. Then she asked more probing questions—determining, it seemed, my level of depression. I admit to not admitting its depths to her, which might have taken *therapy* into a tangential path. The first step was to tell my story, the whole story, and I saved that for the next session the following week.

The second session started out very much like the first, except now Mel said, "Tell me about your week." I hadn't done much since I'd last seen her besides reliving the night of the housewarming party, which I desperately wanted to share with her. I needed someone to understand, or at least to see if she *could* understand. Not wanting to come across as petulant or sound obsessive, I accommodated her by talking about my ongoing job search. Without prompting and before she could steer the conversation elsewhere, I began to unspool the events of December 18, 1999. I went on for five minutes before she stopped me.

Mel grabbed a black book from her desk, a five-by-eight-inch journal, and handed it to me. She instructed me to write out everything that had happened. It felt a bit like being back in school, and reflexively I asked how many pages she wanted. "As much detail as you feel you need, Stephen," she told me. "That's what is important."

When I got home, I started writing. I could hardly stop, and when I had finished, the entire journal had been taken up by my scribble. It took three days, and it covered more than just that night.

The following day, I canceled the remaining therapy sessions. I can't explain how, but the obsession, the guilt from the calamity, the physical pain that I couldn't shake, that relentless ache between my heart and gut—all of it vanished.

It was all gone, miraculously. Of course it would surface briefly every once in a while, when I was reminded of it by this thing or that. And then I would wonder, *Did that really happen? Or was it all a bad dream or a fictional account of a true story? Or was it part of a different me in the infinite fragments of me—like the Ship of Theseus—so far removed that it was really somebody else?* . . . It'd float around in my head for a while, like a nagging song that never seems to go away until it finally does. But holding eighty-pound stock, inviting me to a party in 1999, the tragedy is impossible to dismiss.

Chapter One

December 1999

JOHN ANSWERED THE PHONE with a yawn that stretched into two yawns. I was ringing him up at work on a Monday morning.

"Am I keeping you awake?" I said.

"Just tired, man."

A conversation that I'd had ten minutes earlier in the break room lingered with me. It was with a coworker I barely knew, someone I'd seen around the office for years but whose name I didn't know. We were roughly the same age, mid-thirties, and as a new pot of coffee brewed, we talked about our perceptions of the year 2000 when we were young.

"Where did you think we'd be in 2000?" I asked John. "When you were a kid, I mean, what advancements did you think would happen by now?"

"You mean like flying cars?"

"Yeah, exactly."

"Maybe not flying like airplanes, but definitely hovering cars," John said.

"I thought there'd be a moon base."

"Yes. And for sure cancer would be cured."

"I thought so, too," I said. "In fact, I even remember thinking I could start smoking, and it wouldn't matter because they'd cure lung cancer by now."

"I certainly didn't think about the internet as a thing, this whole dot-com craze."

"No. Or the Y2K problem."

"No, definitely not," he said flatly.

He yawned again.

"You sound tired. Didn't you relax this weekend?" I knew he hadn't.

"No. Sometimes I think I just want to live a simple life—be a monk or something."

"Monks don't hold housewarming parties," I said.

"Yeah, I think Mary did mention something about a party." John started typing. I could hear the keys.

"You didn't see the invitation, did you?"

"No, I didn't. Maybe I wasn't invited."

"Well, I know for a fact you haven't seen it."

The clacking on the other end stopped. "Why? Did Mary forget the 'o' again? She hasn't done that in a long time."

I laughed. "I think she knows her own last name by now. No, it's the date."

"Did she put the wrong day?"

"Not that I know of," I said.

"Then what is it?"

"You need to see for yourself. Once you look at the invitation, you'll understand."

"Fine. I'll ask her about it tonight—by the way, you got me into trouble with her."

"With Mary? How? I haven't spoken to her in weeks." Actually, I hadn't spoken to Mary since their wedding two months earlier.

"Remember you told me I shouldn't hire a gardener?"

"No, I told you one of my dad's sayings. 'If you can't mow your own lawn, you have too much lawn.'"

"Right. And I thought that was a good philosophy. So I didn't hire a gardener."

"And how did that get you in trouble with Mary? Are you terrible at mowing?"

"No, it's not the lawn. I just extended the idea."

"Uh-oh. In what way?" I asked.

"So Mary wanted to hire house cleaners, and I told her that if you can't clean your own house you have too much house."

"Oh no . . ."

"Yeah, so she's angry because I told her not to hire house cleaners," he said.

"Just tell her you've changed your mind."

"I can't now. It's the principle. And if I give in, what kind of message does that send?"

"Are you sure you want to be married? I think you can still get it annulled."

John made a terse grunt. "Anyway. She'll get over it."

"Are you all moved in?" I asked.

"Mostly. I mean, all our stuff is unpacked, but we still have furniture arriving in the next few days."

"I was shocked that you actually agreed to a party right now," I said. John liked to be noticed. But only from afar—admired at a distance where he could pretend to be completely oblivious to it all. In fact, he quietly reveled in it.

"Well . . ." He went on to tell me that he did resist when Mary first suggested a small housewarming party. "Just like there is no such thing as a football game lasting five minutes with five minutes on the clock, as she often complains to me, there is no such thing as a *small* party."

"True. But apparently you gave in."

"Sort of. I actually only agreed to Mary's family and a couple of close friends. But no one in her family was going to be around until Christmas weekend. She didn't want to do it after the holidays, so she got upset."

"And *then* you gave in."

He sighed. "Once the party train leaves the station . . ."

When Mary showed him the dessert menu from the bakery, he knew they were past discussing it. He said his finger drifted to the gourmet fruit tarts. "That's what I'm excited about. I love those fruit tarts."

"You know you can buy one any time you want. I'm pretty sure you have enough money."

"No, I can't. It's like going to the movies by yourself. It just doesn't feel right."

I had gone to the movies plenty of times by myself—you get used to it. Maybe too used to it.

"She ended up inviting everyone from her office," he said. "SGF, too."

SGF stood for Stamford, Greco & Faber and was not a law firm. It was a chic and expensive clothing store where Mary used to work. Now she worked for SmartMile, a car guide publisher.

I immediately thought of Mary's friend, Lauren. "Everyone?"

"SmartMile is a pretty small company," he said, not taking my hint. "There are only thirty or so people working there. She felt like she couldn't invite some without offending others, so she left it open to all."

"Good thing she doesn't work at the phone company."

He spurted out a laugh. "True. Anyway, she mostly told people verbally, so if you got a physical invitation, that means you're special."

"Thank God for Mary. She takes care of everything for you—even remembers my birthday."

"I didn't even know you had a birthday."

"Yeah, I try to forget about it. Especially this year." I had just turned thirty-five.

"Me too," John said. His thirty-fifth birthday was coming up soon.

"You'll be there, right? Six o'clock." A tinge of tenseness laced his voice. For all the pretenses around not inviting anyone (except for one person—as I found out later), I could tell he wanted a friendly face there.

"Sure, I'll be there—for the fruit tarts at least," I said.

"Yeah, exactly—oh, I nearly forgot to tell you!" I heard him slap his desk. "I've got something for you."

"Yeah? What is it?"

"It's a surprise. You're gonna be floored. I'll give it to you at the party."

"No need to bribe me. I'll be there."

"You are going to be so blown away by this, Steve. I promise."

I think he expected me to beg for more details. But I didn't. "Can't wait."

"All right, see you in a couple of weeks, then."

"Or in another hundred years," I said and hung up the phone. I was referring to the two-digit year on the invitation. For anyone involved in fixing the Y2K problem, it was a sin to ever write the ambiguous two-digit year. So I knew John hadn't seen the invitation before it was mailed out.

Chapter Two

March 1994

UNDER THE ANTISEPTIC GLOW of fluorescent lights, a man with pasty skin and flushed cheeks, his floppy brown hair long overdue for a barber's visit, stood in front of the room laying out the extent of the problem. His slightly gravelly voice defied his boyish features. He wrote on the freestanding whiteboard, drawing boxes over here and over there, boxes that represented systems and applications, filled in with acronyms and names: DXL. Otap-LUX, Phoenix-01, Phoenix-02, MTRS... Lines whizzed this way and that, to and fro, between applications and systems. And in the center, a big, puffy cloud. When he was all done, it resembled the big bang.

John Goertz, hired as an information systems manager, was a couple of months into his job when he gathered twenty of us to explain his new raison d'être. It had annoyed me greatly, how he had arranged this meeting, ignoring the specific, unwritten protocols of the phone company. This meeting should have taken weeks, if not months, to set up, the culmination of a dozen or more pre-meetings, starting with me and a few other managers. Then, assuming he had our buy-in, he should have waited for us to discuss with our supervisors before moving forward with the next meeting, and so on, up the chain. Instead Goertz had called the CIO's secretary and dragged all of us to this confab. Heck, I had witnessed an engineer clipping his toenails during a meeting earlier that week and that had been less gauche.

My eyes wandered the room, waiting for someone higher up than me to put this new guy in his place. When Goertz said with solemn despair, "Even if we start today, I'm not sure there is enough time to fix this year 2000 problem," I cracked a laugh. No one else joined in, and I coiled in my seat. But it was barely spring 1994, and this guy was seriously forewarning us about the end of the company—and the entire world!—over two digits.

"Now for an illustration," he said. He pointed at me and asked that I come up to the front of the room. Me? A volunteer in this guy's carnival act? No way! But that would have made me instantly disagreeable to the higher-ups in the room, so as everyone stared at me, I begrudgingly went forward. He directed me to a black laptop on the table, which he opened.

Why did John Goertz have a laptop? Laptops were reserved for vice presidents and above. It was a model that I had seen recently, amazingly small with a large eighty-megabyte-capacity hard drive—and it only weighed five pounds!

"Would you please change the system date to December 31, 1999, eleven fifty-five p.m., and then shut down the computer," Goertz said.

Using the TrackPoint, I unskillfully zigzagged the cursor around the screen until I corralled it to the control panel. I changed the date as directed and shut off the computer. Goertz thanked me and said, "We'll check back in a few minutes." I returned to my seat.

Goertz then started writing numbers on the board under the word *Inventory*. "We have somewhere around two hundred separate applications at the company. In fact, we don't even know the exact number. Nobody knows. And when I started asking the business units, most responded with estimates. But anyway, let's assume, on average, one thousand modules per application. That means we have somewhere around two hundred thousand modules to be reviewed. A good programmer doing nothing but reviewing code all day could probably go through a module in about three or four days. Now, that's a lot of man-hours. So you might be thinking, 'Okay, John, but there's plenty of time still.' But I'd say it's a problem of organization. And decisions have to be made. We might not have the source code. There are parts of programs here coded in the 1970s. Do we rewrite applications? Do we scrap some applications that aren't needed anymore? All of this needs to be assessed."

He was losing the crowd here, so he asked me to come back up to the front and power up the computer. "Any guesses as to what the date is?"

Someone said, "Stuck on December 31, 1999." Someone else guessed January 1, 1900. Another said January 1, 1970.

"What date does it say?" he asked me.

I had to look at it twice. "January 4, 1980."

There was uneasy laughter from the group.

"January 4, 1980," Goertz repeated. "So it's not just our internal code. It's operating systems, embedded systems inside computers, third-party applications. It's hardware. It's all those things. They all have to be inventoried and updated well before the year 2000 . . . Tick-tock." And with that, he concluded his presentation.

I sat back down. The chief information officer, Rex Clifton, a man in his late fifties with perfectly coiffed silver hair, seemingly plucked out of a Washington, DC, committee, stood up and started for the front of the room. Yes! John Goertz was about to be put in his place. Of course, it'd be wrapped in cordial business concepts of collaboration, processes, and culture with a courteous nod to "thinking outside the box"—but John Goertz was about to get it.

Goertz had remained standing, shuffling away from the center of the room until his back was up against the conference room wall. I nearly felt sorry for the guy because he didn't know any better—but then again, he should have. He should have taken the time to learn the convoluted ways of this company. Learn the lay of the land before summoning us all to his dour and daunting presentation, especially right before lunch. Tick-tock. I was getting hungry. Pizza sounded good.

Mr. Clifton stared at the whiteboard for a second, rubbed his chin, and then said, "I think you'll all agree that this was an extremely informative and eye-opening presentation." Everyone around the room nodded. "And I see the need to put more organization around this right away. So I'm putting you in charge of this," Clifton said, looking at Goertz. "Reporting directly to me."

For a few seconds, I looked from one to the other, wondering if this was some kind of elaborate office theater concocted between them for our benefit. I mean, surely Mr. Clifton wouldn't make such a significant move without serious thought and further input from his direct reports. Not to mention discussions with his counterparts at the business units.

A barely perceptible, self-satisfied smile on Goertz's face gave him away. This was his master plan all along. Point out this ridiculous problem, scare everyone, and get himself a promotion. And all I wanted to do at that moment was to punch him in the mouth—and then go get a slice of pepperoni-and-mushroom pizza from the cafeteria.

The CIO turned to my boss's boss, who ran corporate information technology. "Woody, you need to put together a dedicated team to support this. This is going to require a lot of new expenditures, and you need to add this to your budget for next year." A budget that already exceeded two hundred million dollars.

The Year 2000 Conversion Team was born, and it became my task to be a service delivery manager for every corporate system related to the project. Though I would not be reporting directly to Goertz, I'd be attending a lot of his team meetings. He'd hold quite a bit of power over my work agenda and some say in my performance evaluations.

That afternoon, after eating an abandoned, cellophane-wrapped sandwich from the break room, I visited Henry

Renfro at his third-floor cubicle. From Henry's desk some of the best views of the man-made lake on campus were to be had. Henry had been at the phone company since graduating college and was now a few short years from retirement, living out his flagging career in corporate finance. He had previously worked in the billing systems department as a COBOL programmer, moving up the salary grades over the years. In his early forties, he transferred to a group that was responsible for the company's financial reporting systems, and eventually he settled as a mid-level manager in finance. From an era when large companies provided incentives for employees to spend their entire career with them, Henry was one of the last. Not much later, the company restructured its pension plan, which had vested heavily and generously toward the end of one's tenure. The restructured plan funded more evenly—and less generously—throughout someone's career.

Henry gave off a bohemian vibe, with his gray beard and his easygoing devotion to his stained glass artwork. He always dispensed sage, if not comedic, advice. When I told him about the meeting, he chuckled. "We had this problem in the late seventies," he said in his soft, raspy voice. With his scraggly beard and gentle manners, Henry reminded me of a well-worn teddy bear. He explained that they used to code the year with one digit to save memory. "Eight columns on the punched card for sorting, one digit was significant." He shook his head. "We should have fixed the year to four digits a lot earlier, but who would have guessed that programs from the early eighties would still be running today?"

With Henry's confirmation of Goertz's assertion, I deepened my knowledge of the year 2000 problem. I read an article in a computer magazine and quickly became a convert. Factories could shut down. Elevators could get stuck. Nuclear power plants could fail catastrophically. And there was proof of this problem already. A 104-year-old woman in Minnesota had gotten a notice to attend preschool. This was not an inconsequential dilemma, this was a fated apocalypse wrapped in a bow of irony. Mankind's progress would cause its own demise over two simple digits. The most undeveloped parts of the world wouldn't notice; the most advanced economies could collapse into complete chaos. The structures that kept society civilized were fragile indeed.

Soon after I started telling my friends back in Ohio about it. But they mocked me. "Come on, why would my car have a problem? It doesn't have a date except the clock that always tells the wrong time anyway," my college roommate said. Realizing that I sounded a bit crazed, like an end-of-days alarmist, I stopped talking about it until the media picked up on it several years later.

It was a couple of weeks after that seminal meeting when I saw John Goertz again. Except this time it was in his new office, Goertz having officially transferred to his new role: director, year 2000 compliance. His hair was neat and he wore an oat-colored tweed jacket that he might have borrowed from his father. His desk was perfectly clean, though he still hadn't unpacked his boxes. I stared at the boxes. There were three of them sitting on the floor, and I wondered how anyone could have accumulated so many papers in such a short amount of time working there.

We had no official agenda to review. The meeting was an informal get-together in my new capacity as service delivery manager for the Year 2000 team—a team with no one on it except John Goertz. I became a sort of liaison between the Year 2000 team and corporate information technology. I would be involved in ensuring year 2000 compliance with any new IT project and procuring replacement of noncompliant systems under the corporate IT umbrella.

Despite being on board with the year 2000 problem, I still didn't care for John. People our age weren't supposed to have director titles. The average age of a director at the company was at least forty-five. Barely a manager, I felt inferior to him, and after I sat down, I consciously avoided crossing my arms. I firmly gripped the chair as if I were about to be tossed about on a roller coaster.

"I'm kind of tired of the cafeteria," he said. "You like Chinese food?"

It was barely eleven o'clock. "Sure, but—"

"Where can you get good Chinese food around here?"

"Depends on what you mean by 'around here.' The best place I know of is on the other side of the bay."

"Great, let's go." He stood up and removed his jacket, setting it on the back of his chair. "You don't have lunch plans, do you?"

"No, but it'll take like thirty minutes just to get there." Or more. It was across the bridge and up the peninsula a few miles.

"Perfect. I'll drive."

On our way in John's baby-blue BMW, he asked me whether he had "rubbed some people the wrong way." At first I thought it might be an underhanded dig at me, but then he added that a finance director for one of the business units had sent him "a terse ALL-IN-1." ALL-IN-1 was the email application we used.

"I don't know," I said. "I don't really know him." I hadn't really heard anyone talking badly about John—unless you include the back-and-forth with myself. "Maybe he doesn't like the color of your car."

"Huh?" he said, then laughed. "Oh yeah. I know. It's awful. But I got such a great deal on this thing, it was hard to pass up."

I suddenly didn't hate him so much, with his disarming ability to laugh at himself.

"Where are you from originally?" I asked. I had pegged him as a Midwesterner, Upper Midwest. Not Wisconsin or Minnesota—no obvious elongated vowels. And not Indiana, either—not deliberate enough. He was from Michigan, Ohio, or Illinois.

"You don't think I'm native Californian?"

"No one is."

He chuckled. "Ohio, actually."

"Me too. Whereabouts?"

As it turned out, we had perfectly missed each other when we lived in the Buckeye State. Both of us had graduated high school in 1983. He was from Athens and went to college at the University of Toledo. I was from Toledo—technically, Holland, a small town outside of Toledo—and went to school at Ohio University, where his father taught Russian literature. I missed his father, too, as I got my degree in electrical engineering and got nowhere near Gordy Hall. We both moved to California right after college, seeking warmer winters and proximity to leading-edge technology.

Over lunch he asked me my opinion about hiring a team. "What's best, hiring from within or doing an external search?"

Rex Clifton had once described the phone company as steering a herd of elephants, difficult to maneuver, but once turned, unstoppable. I repeated this line to him without attributing credit.

"So what you're saying is, if I hire within, the project will be slow off the blocks?"

"Yes, but eventually you'll be moving. If you hire from outside, you're likely to get some initial traction, but you'll eventually encounter pushback and you'll need those veteran soft skills. I'd hire a mix. What's your budgeted headcount?"

"I don't know yet, but I'm hoping for six."

"Go half-and-half. That would be the best bet. Regardless, you'll have to post any position internally first before you're allowed to look outside."

He nodded with an appreciative and understanding grimace on his face.

By the end of our lunch, I had really warmed up to John—he was a friendly, down-to-earth guy who, sure, was looking for career advancement, but he was no longer the prick who had called all of us together that day to play systems Pictionary. In fact, he had explained that when his boss had resigned—after one month of John being there—John had discussed all of it with him. His boss's advice: call a meeting with the CIO, and everyone else. "He gave me the list of people to invite," John said. I thought it must have been an intentional joke—a time bomb laid by his boss, though I didn't tell John that.

So far we had common backgrounds and he was receptive to suggestions—heck, soliciting suggestions—yet our bond wasn't complete until we were back in the building. It was Joanna, a twenty-two-year-old admin, who completed our friendship. As we were walking down the hallway after returning from lunch, Joanna walked past us.

"Who's the Swede?" he asked as we ducked into his office.

"Swede?" I said. "You know, not all blondes are Swedish." Joanna's blond hair wasn't hers—too perfect, a flawless flaxen, a shade shy of pure porn-star platinum.

He explained that *Swede* was the nickname he gave any attractive woman—blond or not. John numbered his Swedes sequentially, and Joanna took on "Swede 7."

"Do you know her?" he asked me.

I didn't let on about the extent to which I had tracked Joanna, fearing he would label me a stalker. Joanna was a secretary for one of the midlevel executives who had a knack for hiring women like Joanna. Unfortunately, most never lasted more than a few months, except Joanna, who had surpassed her expiration date by a year. There were rumors she was a model for those bodice-ripping romance covers, but I had yet to confirm it—and not for lack of trying. Every time I went to the library, when no one else was around, I spun through the paperback turnstiles full of trash novels, dizzily searching for Joanna.

"I think she's an office admin, for one of the directors or vice presidents," is all I said about Joanna, Swede 7.

Chapter Three

Spring 1995

THE ONLY DIFFERENCE between the gray walls of my cubicle and a prison cell was that a prison cell had more comforts, a bed to lie down in, and even more space. Sure, I was allowed to leave my cube or quit my job at any time, but in reality I was hooked to a certain lifestyle and ambitions that required me to work in an office. And despite the camaraderie and friendship that John and I had developed over the previous year, being around him depressed me. He had the better job, nicer car, the house—well, townhouse in Pleasanton. I still rented a one-bedroom apartment five miles from the office. And even though John never flaunted those things, something inside of me felt the need to one-up him on something.

One day John told me about a new Swede he had met, Swede 8, a "new girl in marketing." Had I seen her? No, but I wondered what Mr. Year 2000 was doing hanging around marketing. The marketing department was on the other side of the building on the fourth floor, nowhere near us. Before I started poking around, I needed a name. And even though I asked with a disinterested frown, he shook his head. "Nope. I don't need the extra competition." Game on!

So I made a beeline to the third floor to see Henry Renfro. Since he worked in finance, I thought he might have access to headcount information and personnel files.

Henry and I small-talked for a minute, and then he told me about his latest stained glass project and his new endeavor. He was about to start teaching a class on it at a local community college. A ten-minute conversation ensued on whether stained glass was considered art or craft. But unlike our recent back-and-forth on what constituted a sport ("Anything you can bet on," had been my glib answer), this was more one-sided—I didn't have much of an opinion on the subject.

In an awkward segue, I asked him if he knew about someone new in the marketing department.

"Corporate marketing?" He shook his head. "No. Why would I?"

"I thought maybe you had access to that kind of information."

"No, not me. I'm not that important. What's this about?"

I told him it had to do with John Goertz, that he was being coy about someone he had met.

"My advice is, don't get your butter where you get your bread," he said.

I nodded quickly. "Yep. Good advice."

He scratched hard at his beard. "You know, Megan might be able to help you."

Megan Stanton was the controller for our business unit, and there was no way I was going to ask her. I thanked Henry and went back to my desk.

From a distance, Megan extracted optimism from any man checking. Shoulder-length, thick golden hair and a sleek, athletic build, a body that made the top ten of any loose gathering of men after—or heck, even during—work. But that was it. She was certainly not a Swede, and the tight lines that appeared on her cheeks when she smiled made our five-year age gap seem even wider.

No one was supposed to know about Megan and me, especially John. I wasn't entirely proud of our relationship. Not only was Megan not a Swede, she was still married—though separated and actively pursuing a divorce.

For the last few months, Megan and I had been sneaking out of work early and meeting at my apartment. She always left before six to pick up her son. But the realization that her divorce would soon be finalized had brought about extra phone calls and more than a few tears. I wanted nothing to do with her anguish. Sure, it was cruel on my part, but in my defense, it was Megan who had said she wasn't looking to get involved in a committed relationship any time soon.

About twenty minutes after seeing Henry, I got a call from him. "Tiffany Popiel," he said.

"How did you find out?"

"I know people who know people," he said.

"Well, thanks. I owe you lunch."

It wasn't until the following week that I officially broke it off with Megan, and it took me that long to "run into" Tiffany Popiel.

Tiffany Popiel was pale skinned, translucent I daresay; light blond haired; and mostly a beanpole. She was tall, nearly six feet, give or take a half inch, though I didn't know that when I first saw her. Sauntering through the marketing department, I saw that her cubicle was one away from the main aisle, and from there I could only gather her general features. I didn't see her whole face, only her profile, and I should have questioned John's call here—except that she might actually have been part Swedish. Still, I went with it because my ultimate goal was to beat John Goertz at something.

My plan to meet Tiffany involved the corporate-subsidized cafeteria, which was the lunch destination for most employees. The food court there wasn't half bad, offering a variety of options, from burgers and fries to international cuisine of the month. A limited breakfast was available, too, but not many people had breakfast at work. It took me three days of staggered lunches to find Tiffany, who arrived at 11:50 and landed at the salad bar.

Tiffany was even thinner than I had figured, flat-chested, and except for her white eyelashes, prettier than her profile had let on. She had a slightly unsteady gait, like a filly not quite used to its legs. Despite my misgivings about the Swede moniker, I waited for her around the same time the next day, hoping for consistency. And that she was. As I wandered around from station to station, not only did she arrive at 11:50, she went straight to the salad bar again. I normally found a salad unsatisfying for lunch, but I eased next to her and said, "Hi."

She smiled and said, "Hello," back and kept on building a salad.

"You're new, right?"

She nodded. "Yeah, a little over a month now." She stuck out her hand. "I'm Tiffany. I'm a marketing analyst."

It was at this point that I became aware of her peculiar eyes. Her left eye was light blue and her right eye was hazel.

"Steve," I said, shaking her hand. "I'm in IT service delivery."

We swapped pleasantries, and grabbing a Styrofoam box, I said, "I love this salad bar."

She nodded. "Yeah, it's pretty good. Though I wish they had beets."

Who liked beets? "Yeah," I said agreeably. "We should mention it to someone."

We built our salads and headed to the register together—or rather, I hurriedly finished mine and chased after her. After she paid, I said, "Maybe I'll see you again tomorrow at the salad bar." She nodded, smiled a bit mechanically, and left.

After a couple more days of eating salads, I asked her to join me at one of the tables. She hesitated for a moment and then said, "Yeah, I guess I have a little time."

Her heterochromia was a bit disconcerting at first. I forced eye contact with her even though I had an urge to look away. I found her eyes to be both freakish and oddly alluring.

There was another week of drenching my salad with more

and more dressing, and we sat together a few times. After we had successfully lobbied the manager of the cafeteria to add beets to their salad bar, I was obligated to eat beets. I convinced myself that I really liked her, and I even started to enjoy beets.

Finally I asked her out, and she agreed. I hadn't mentioned any of this to John, saving it as a surprise—a punch to his gut!

At a nearby restaurant, Tiffany and I had drinks after work. I found out that she hadn't even heard of—or at least didn't remember—John Goertz. A victorious feeling swelled in me.

The following morning I sauntered over to John's office, but he wasn't there. So I went up to see Henry. Since I had promised him lunch, I wanted to see what day he might be available.

"Did you meet Tiffany?" Henry asked.

"Yes, I did."

"Is John still going out with her?"

"Going out?" I laughed. "She doesn't even remember meeting him."

"Uh-oh," he said. "I think I know what you're up to."

I stuttered for a second and then admitted that I had run into her in the cafeteria. I quickly pivoted to politics.

Henry liked talking politics almost as much as he liked stained glass. Before I knew better, I would have pegged him to lean somewhat hippie-left. But more than anything else, he held to the importance of in-state politics. "Democracy," he once argued, "wanes the farther away it is from local control. It eventually gets diluted to mean almost nothing." He believed voters in each state should decide their own government: "If Louisiana wants to ban abortion, why should I in California tell them what to do?"

I brought up a Supreme Court decision that had been handed down that day. The court had struck down state laws that created term limits for congressional candidates.

As if I were a student visiting a poli-sci professor during office hours, Henry gestured for me to sit down on the hard wooden chair in his cubicle. "That case was decided by five to four. Decisions that close are bad for the country."

"Sure, but how do you fix it?" I asked. "It's a divided court."

Henry rubbed his hands together. He explained his idea, which involved a supermajority. Since an amendment to the Constitution requires ratification by three-quarters of the states, he argued, why not apply that same standard to the court? "Seven justices on the Supreme Court have to agree in order to override a state law. Federal cases would remain a simple majority," he said.

The idea was intriguing. I asked him about *Roe v. Wade.* Would abortion have remained up to the states with his supermajority requirement? No, he said. That was a seven–two decision.

Having had my fill of politics and constitutional law, on the way back to my desk, I passed by John's office again. He was leaning comfortably back in his chair, his hands laced behind his head, watching as a woman wrote something on the whiteboard. She had straight, shoulder-length blond hair and a sweater that stretched in the right places.

Judging by her profile and figure, I nearly interrupted just to get introduced. Instead I snuck John a two-fingered wave as I breezed by. He called me back. "Hey, Steve! Come here for a sec."

As I entered, my heart thumped. This woman gave Joanna a run for her money. I dislike the heady tenseness that a striking woman extracts from me. Instantly I felt nervous.

"This is Julie. She just started here a few weeks ago in corporate communications."

"Corporate communications?" I mumbled.

She smiled at me as we shook hands. I glanced over at John, who flashed eight fingers. He then explained that Rex Clifton had suggested leveraging corporate communications to get the word out company-wide about the year 2000 problem, an awareness campaign. "Julie was just telling me that 'year 2000 problem' sounds dull. We need a more attention-grabbing headline. 'Y2K' is starting to gain traction."

There was a certain irony to abbreviating 2000 to Y2K when shortening the year was the cause of the whole damn problem in the first place.

"It's catchy," she said. "'The Y2K bug.'"

"It's not really a bug," I said.

"No, technically not," John said. "But for people to understand it, it works."

I nodded, smiled pleasantly, and excused myself. I had to break up with Tiffany before lunch. No burger would ever taste any better.

Chapter Four

February 1998

WHITE LIGHTS TWINKLED over the windows—perhaps Christmas remnants or else this place was always festive. John and I met at Moe's Way, a casually pretentious restaurant near an outdoor mall in Palo Alto. It was a Thursday night in early February 1998. I hadn't seen or spoken much to John in over a month. At the beginning of the year, he had left the phone company to join a start-up in Mountain View.

When John quit the phone company, he told me he was quitting for a couple of reasons. With new management looking over his shoulder, he'd never be able to manage the Y2K program like he had before the takeover. And he reasoned that if he didn't leave soon, he'd have to see it all the way through. No one would hire him in 1999, with the end being so near—"What would that say about my character if I quit so close to the finish line?"

We sat down, and after ordering red wine, John began to tell me about the craziness inside this new dot-com world. "People bring their dogs to the office."

"Seriously?"

He nodded. "There are always five or six dogs around. The other day I had to step over one to get to my desk."

"You don't have an office?"

He shook his head. "Nobody does, not even the CEO. I mean, there are conference rooms if you have a meeting or need to make a private call."

"Too bad you don't have a dog," I said. "Remember when you got in trouble for bringing in a plant to work?"

"Oh yeah," he said, chuckling. A few weeks after John moved into his office, he brought in a five-foot ficus tree. The facilities manager complained that he wasn't allowed to do that without approval since all plants in offices and common areas were maintained by a company-paid gardener.

"All sounds pretty good," I said. "Except the dogs. I like dogs but . . ."

"Oh, free lunches catered every day, too. And all the snacks and soda you can eat."

"Is the pay comparable?"

"Not as good. But they gave me a lot of options. Fifty thousand."

Not too long before that, options had been a foreign concept to me, given exclusively to executives. It was a few weeks earlier that the company, having recently been taken over by a Texas-based entity, had announced that our tangible annual bonus would be swapped for options. I received a few hundred shares. So fifty thousand sounded fantastic. "Wow!"

"Hopefully it will be worth something," he said. "I guess I could have taken the hospital job and kept the same salary and a stable job. And it's important work, but . . ." A large hospital group had made John an offer to take charge of their back-office systems. But his primary task would have been to ensure Y2K compliance, and he wanted to put Y2K behind him.

"But what?" I asked.

"The reality is that there's zero chance to make a killing at a hospital," he said.

I laughed. "You mean a hundred percent chance."

"Huh?"

"To make a killing. At a hospital . . ."

He smiled. "Yeah, wrong word. But seriously, there's a chance at this company. It could mean a lot of money."

Once he had finished describing all the other distractions at the start-up (like ping-pong, foosball, and darts), we checked out the one-page dinner menu. I had been keeping an eye on a tied Rangers-Kings game playing over John's shoulder, but then the bartender changed the channel to a basketball game where I wasn't carrying any action.

As the waitress came our way, John said he was going to order the hanger steak, which was what I had planned to get. Unwilling to copy John, I was left to decide on something else, though really there wasn't much of a choice at all. With five entrées on the overpriced menu, I wasn't about to order the thirty-five-dollar Kobe beef from SR Ranch, wherever that was, or the Moroccan lamb with goat-cheese truffled potatoes for thirty-two. Since spicy foods often unsettle my stomach, I skipped over the Thai chicken. So that left the applewood-smoked pork chop, and I was going to pick that, but a pork chop really paled in comparison to the steak. "I'll have that, too," I finally said, except instead of a Caesar salad, I ordered the organic salad, which came with "heirloom" tomatoes—probably kissed by the goddess Pomona.

John turned around and saw the game on the television. "You got anything riding on that game?" He had taken a peculiar interest in my gambling lately, and I didn't know exactly why. He wasn't interested in sports betting.

"Nope," I said without mentioning the hockey game.

I didn't necessarily hide it from him, though I wasn't entirely forthcoming, either. He had a slight contempt for sports betting, so I didn't tell him the extent of it, the number of people at work who were seeing me to place bets on their behalf. By my vague descriptions—*I won/lost a few bucks last night*—he probably thought I was putting down ten or twenty on a few games here and there. The truth was I was regularly wagering a hundred a day, two to three times during the week, and several hundred on football games on the weekend. That didn't even include another few hundred for coworkers, who'd ask me to place bets with my bookie, usually for football. At one point I even considered becoming an agent with my bookmaker. But I was afraid of being caught by management and losing my job.

"You still betting regularly?" It wasn't like I had asked him for a loan, so I didn't understand the source of his concern.

I nodded and pleasantly answered: "Sure, sometimes."

His mouth eased into a crooked smile. "You know, when we first met, for the first couple months I thought you might be bipolar."

"Bipolar?" I let out a little laugh.

"Yeah. You'd come in, especially after the weekend, really high or really low. You'd be like, 'Hey, let's go to lunch, I'm buying,' or you'd be really quiet. And then you told me about the betting, and it all made sense. Your mood was dependent on how you fared."

I shrugged, a little annoyed. I didn't think I was like that at all. Steering the conversation away, I blurted a joke that Henry Renfro had told me that day.

John, who despised all politics, smiled lightly and huffed a token laugh.

Sitting there with the lingering joke, knowing that we wouldn't be discussing the latest political scandal, I quickly realized that John and I didn't have much in common. He sat there wearing blue jeans and a slim gray V-neck sweater over a white shirt, while I wore the standard business-casual flair—one of my half dozen button-down collared shirts tucked into my Dockers. Realizing that the thing we bonded over was the place we worked together—or at least used to—I recalled something about F. Jake that I wanted to tell him.

Jake Fitzgerald, or F. Jake as we called him, was part of the Year 2000 Compliance group and had reported to John for a few years. A curator of implausibilities and misadventures, F. Jake had earned his moniker after claiming he was related to F. Scott Fitzgerald. We didn't believe him, and neither did we believe most of the outlandish stories regularly thrown our way.

"They offered F. Jake your job," I said.

"That doesn't surprise me. He gets along awfully well with those boys from San Antonio."

"I swear he adds a slight drawl whenever he speaks to them."

"Pretty soon he'll be wearing cowboy boots to work. So he's the new director, huh?" There was an edge to his tone. As if F. Jake wasn't worthy—or, more accurately, as if nobody was worthy.

"No, he didn't take it."

"What? Why not?"

"This is the good part," I said. "He claims he briefly dated Jessica."

Jessica was John's admin for a few weeks. She was in her late forties, attractive. One of those women fighting hard against being middle-aged—always well made up and always on the latest fad diet. She had long, chestnut-brown hair that lacked that youthful sheen and smoothness. She wasn't making the cover of romance novels, but could she have been twenty years and two kids earlier? Maybe.

"When? I didn't know that," John said with a doubtful glare.

"Apparently they hit it off and went out a couple times."

His eyes narrowed and his brow wrinkled. "That's not right. He should have asked me first—well, at least told me about it."

"Why? You hired Jessica and then gave your notice a week later."

"True," he said, relenting. "But what does dating Jessica have to do with not taking the job? Because he'd be her boss?"

"Yeah. How awkward would that be?" I said.

"I suppose, though he could've tried finding her another position. She was quite capable from what I could tell."

"He should have traded Jessica for Swede 7!"

John smiled and shook his head. "They're not baseball cards."

"How awesome would that have been?" I said, ignoring his reproof.

He kept shaking his head. "There's no way Swede 7 would have agreed."

"Maybe. Maybe not."

"Definitely not," he said.

"I guess we'll never know."

After dinner, we crossed the parking lot to an outdoor mall. There was no destination in mind, we were just hoping to walk off the meal. The night air carried a gentle chill that felt good. We lapped the outside of the mall, which was mostly restaurants and luxury department stores, and at one point we crossed into the interior pathways. Not many people were strolling about, and the stores—mostly women's clothing—appeared to be closing soon.

Passing by one such boutique, I spotted a blond-haired trap with a body and haute couture that belonged on a runway. Her thick, straight hair glistened under the store's bright lights. I slowed the pace, nudging John in the ribs with my elbow.

"Check out the Swede in the window over there," I said.

John glanced over. The Swede was fidgeting through a rack of glittering dresses. "Yeah. Wow."

"Go in there and talk to her."

"Yeah, right," he said sarcastically.

"I dare you," I said with childish fervor.

He looked at me and then said, "Double-dog dare?"

I laughed. "Sure, double-dog dare. Whatever it takes."

He darted toward the entrance. A big smile awaited him when he stopped and turned around. But he didn't. Without hesitation, not even a glance back at me, he entered the store. How much had he had to drink? Not more than me, and I certainly wouldn't have gone in there. But every once in a while John surprised me and did something unexpected.

I edged back toward a tree, planted in a respite of concrete and aggregate with a good view. The Swede, meanwhile, had shifted over to a mannequin wearing a red cocktail dress. As I thought about how good she'd look in it, she unceremoniously disrobed the mannequin. I was a little stunned; it took me a long second to comprehend it all, and suddenly feeling self-conscious—a creep staring at a naked plastic woman—I shoved my hands into my pockets and walked away.

Nearing the door of Stamford, Greco & Faber, wondering what had happened to John, I spotted him through the window, engaged with a brunette. Pretty enough, though I couldn't really tell for sure from that distance. Certainly not stunning in the way of the billboard blonde. I watched as she pulled out what appeared to be a black sweater and held it out for John to see. He said something, and she put it up against herself—a high neckline. John nodded emphatically.

Deciding to wait for him a few stores down, I sat on a cold bench. When John came out, he came out holding the handle of a large white bag in his hand. His eyes roved the mall until he saw me.

"You buying women's clothing now?" I said, standing up when he reached me. The bag had *SGF* on it in big block letters.

"Let's go," he said without stopping.

"What happened?"

He blindly handed me the receipt. He had spent $125.74. "Turn it over," he said. On the other side was a phone number with a name above it: Mary.

"The brunette who helped you?"

"Yeah. When I went in there, I started for the Swede, and then this one popped up from the back asking me if I needed help. I said I was looking for something for my sister—that's all I could come up with on the spot. She said she would help me."

I pointed at the bag. "And that's for your sister?" I put air quotes around *sister*. He didn't have a sister.

He laughed. "Yeah. She was cute. Not exactly a Swede, but that blonde would have blown me off in an instant anyway."

"She works there, you know."

"Who?"

"The blonde."

"How do you know?"

"Customers generally don't disrobe mannequins."

He laughed. "Well, at least I got Mary's number out of it."

"So you're going to ask her out?"

He nodded. "Yeah, I think so. Why not?"

"When you get married, she'll be surprised to find out you don't have a sister."

"No," he said. "She'll be flattered because I'll tell her that I made that up to meet her."

"Except you really went in there to meet the Swede."

He looked at me with a mischievous smile. "She'll never know that."

Chapter Five

NOT LONG AFTER JOHN AND I had our dinner in Palo Alto, he and Mary went out on their first date. They went to Cogge's Restaurant in Los Gatos, which wasn't far from Mary's apartment in Campbell. During dinner, Mary asked John how his sister had liked the black cashmere sweater. John nervously admitted that he didn't have a sister and that he'd gone in there to meet her.

"Really?" Mary said. "Most guys go in there to meet Lauren."

"Who's Lauren?" he asked innocently.

Not only did Mary work with Lauren, they were roommates. They talked about Lauren for a while. Lauren's father, a successful and rather high-profile criminal defense attorney, had died when she was a freshman in high school. The family's fortunes changed considerably. "Believe me, she wouldn't be working at SGF and sharing an apartment with me in Campbell if her father were still alive."

"Where would she be?"

"San Francisco, probably. And definitely not working unless it suited her."

"Aren't you best friends?"

Mary admitted that they were close, that they shared everything, that they knew everything about each other. Mary had befriended Lauren at the public high school they attended. "But we've spent *way* too much time together over the last couple of years, between work and home. People need a break from each other."

At the end of dinner, as they walked among the closed shops and open restaurants and active bars, Mary mentioned that Cogge's used to be a funeral home.

"What!" John exclaimed. Until John told me this story, I didn't know either: he had a phobia of anything related to dead people, whether it be a cemetery or objects—jewelry, clothing, furniture—that had belonged to (or "belongs to," as John put it) dead people. Shopping at an antique store was like rummaging through a cemetery garage sale.

Mary laughed at this, and then, staring at John (who said his face must have paled), grabbed his hand. They held hands the rest of the evening strolling through town.

About a month or so after that, so somewhere in early spring when the weather should have been perfectly sunny but instead was quite wet that year, John invited me over to his house for dinner. "We have something important to tell you."

"'We' who?" I said, knowing that he meant Mary, whom I had met only once.

"Mary. We want to tell you something. Swede 11, too. The two people closest to us."

It was touching, but more than that, I got nervous. I hadn't met Lauren. My only exposure to her had been a voyeur's view that night through the window at SGF, and, of course, whatever John had told me about her. "Swede 11 will be there?"

"Yeah, it'll be fine. Don't worry, she doesn't bite—well, actually, she does. But we'll be there to protect you."

John had gotten a lot of exposure to Lauren, and he had spoken at length about her. So much so that part of me thought he might be with Mary in order to get close to Lauren, even if most of what he had to say about her had a disparaging edge to it. But that might have been a self-defensive mechanism. After all, beauty hides personality flaws.

It also crossed my mind that they were trying to set me up with Lauren. But immediately I doubted that. Though our rivalry had ended long ago, to some extent a remnant of it remained. Even that night when I had dared him to go into SGF: a) I didn't expect him to actually go in, and b) if he had gotten Lauren's phone number, I would have only pretended to be happy for him. Did John feel the same way? Yes, I thought so, so it was hard to imagine that he'd be part of a scheme to put Lauren and me together.

"Are you and Mary going steady now?" I said jokingly. "Is that the big news?"

"No, no, don't guess. I really want it to be a surprise."

I arrived at John's townhouse a few minutes early with dessert in hand. Mary was in the kitchen working on a salad. John asked if I wanted a drink, which was the reason I had come early. My nerves had me wound tight. Partially from this announcement, whatever it was, but mostly because I was about to meet Lauren. Wine or whiskey, John asked me. I went for what worked fast, no ice, even though I've never had much of a taste for hard alcohol.

"Hi, Mary," I said, setting the cheesecake down on the kitchen counter. At this point I had only seen Mary once before. John and I had repeated our dinner in Palo Alto, except this time after eating we entered SGF without any "double-dog" dares. I met Mary and her coworker Luda (Lauren was not working that night). What struck me the most about that five-minute encounter was Mary's hair—dark, thick, straight hair that went just beyond her shoulders. Her big eyes, a dark brown color, didn't deviate when she was talking to someone. She exuded a certain confidence and perfect cordiality—not too cool and not too casual—that can only be learned from one's parents.

"It's great to see you again, Steve," she said. She waited for me to set the box down and then gave me a hug. I wasn't expecting it, and Mary, being maybe five-two, stretched from her toes to embrace me. "Thank you for bringing dessert."

"Of course." There was a charm about her, but I couldn't tell if it was an act or truly genuine. "Smells good in here. I'm glad you're cooking," I said. "I don't think John even knows how to turn on the stove."

Mary shook her head. "No. John's making the roast."

"What? He orders takeout every night."

"I'm only putting the salad together. He's making the potatoes, too."

"Wow," I said. "Well, I made the cheesecake."

Mary laughed. "I like how you put it in a box from . . ." She looked at it more closely. "Marie's Bakery."

"That's a disguise. I was attempting to be modest."

John came into the kitchen with my drink.

"Is your announcement tonight that you learned how to cook?"

"Ha ha. Yeah, I can cook. I don't really like to cook if it's just me, that's all."

The doorbell rang at precisely six o'clock, and John went to go get it. I stepped out from the kitchen but remained at a distance. Lauren, Swede 11, stood in the doorway. The whole scene went surreal. The last time I had seen her, she was undressing a mannequin. John bent over for a hug. Lauren gave a smirk and said, "Is Mary moving in with you? Is that why I'm here?"

"Patience," he said. "We'll tell you soon enough."

Lauren was as gorgeous in person as from a distance, which surprised me. I'd expected a flaw. Eyes too close together. Thick eyebrows. An awkward nose. A crooked tooth or two. The high expectations of memory were completely met.

She disentangled herself, and gripping a bottle of wine as if holding a duck just shot out of the sky, she eyed me up and down suspiciously. I got the feeling she hadn't been told that I—or rather, someone else, as she didn't know me—was going to be there. My senses suddenly elevated, I got out a husky,

"Hello," that barely got out at all. I cleared my throat, about to try again—

"I'll have one of those," she said, pointing at my glass.

Shutting the door, John turned and said, "That's my good friend Steve. Steve, Lauren."

I tried again. "Hi." This time louder—too loud.

She hardly looked at me and returned an indifferent, "Hey."

She turned to John and said, "I hope you cooked, John, because Mary is an awful cook."

Mary came out. "He-e-e-y," she said in an offended tone.

"Are you a good cook?" I asked Lauren.

Lauren shook her head. "No, but Mary's even worse."

"I'd take that challenge," Mary said.

"Awesome," I said. "John and I can be the judges."

"No, John would be biased. Just you," Lauren said.

"Sure. Just tell me where and when."

John pointed to Lauren. "You serious about that whiskey?"

Lauren nodded. "Why not?" She held out the bottle of wine. "I just brought this to be polite."

Taking the bottle, John gave a little shrug. "All right. Coming right up."

Lauren was in a black halter top and jeans and black slingbacks with a short heel. I had to peel my eyes away from her. I didn't want to be caught in an admiring stare.

John made us wait for dinner, when we had our plates full of prime rib and potatoes, and our glasses filled with wine, before standing up and making the big announcement:

"Mary and I are engaged."

"What!" Lauren said. Her eyes shot to Mary. "Mary Yolanda, are you pregnant?" she said in a maternal tone.

"No, of course not," Mary said.

"Congratulations," I said. "Or best wishes or whatever you're supposed to say." What I really wanted to say to John was, *Are you sure? You only met her a couple of months ago.*

"So you're leaving the apartment and moving in with him," Lauren said with a slack thumb pointing in John's direction. "That's what you're really telling me."

Mary shook her head. "No, we just wanted to tell you our news. We're not moving in together until we get married."

"And when is that?" she asked.

Mary turned to John and shook her head. "We don't know yet. I think maybe summer next year."

Lauren was quiet for a while. Mary and John talked excitedly in a loose, speculative way, about wedding ideas and such. I'd lob in a joke here and there, but I was pretty quiet, too. Then there was a demonstrable change in Lauren. I first noticed it when she got up to get more wine. Mary, telling me the story about how she and John met (apparently, I wasn't there that night), didn't notice Lauren. Lauren's hands brushed up deliberately against John's back as she walked by him. I didn't see his reaction entirely because Mary kept on. My eyes darted to John briefly—he carried an indeterminate smile, possibly bemused, possibly exhilarated, or perhaps both. When I glanced back at him a few seconds later, it had disappeared, his stoic expression back in place.

I have to admit that the rib roast and the oven-crisp, lemony potatoes were quite delicious. I don't know if my opinion was influenced by my low expectations of Chef John. The roast had a tasty herb crust, blackened, and the center was a perfect pink. After dinner, Mary got up to collect the plates. I got up, too, but she shook her head at me and said John would help her. "We'll clean up and get dessert. You two relax."

It was an obvious gesture to leave Lauren and me alone for a bit.

After Mary and John had left, I smiled at Lauren, who didn't reciprocate. We were sitting across from each other. I leaned in and said in a low voice, "Why do you think they're getting engaged so quickly?"

"You don't know?" Lauren didn't bother lowering her voice, but the sound of clanking dishes and running water from the kitchen probably concealed our conversation.

I shook my head. "No. I mean, she's not pregnant, so . . ."

"Mary dated this guy for almost two years, kind of an older guy like John—"

"Early thirties isn't old," I interrupted.

"Are you John's age?"

"Yeah."

"Don't get offended. I said older, not old. You guys are older than us, right?"

I laughed it off. "Sure, right."

"I like older men," she said. "Guys my age are the worst—I mean, they're not men. They're frat boys stretching out their college years."

"What happened between Mary and that guy she dated?"

"When she started talking marriage, he dumped her. So now she pushes the marriage button early in the relationship. I told her most guys were going to run away. But she's afraid of dating for several years and then getting dropped. I guess her strategy worked with John if she got him to commit this fast." She held an imaginary fishing pole in her right hand and with her left made the spinning motion of reeling in a catch.

"Well, that explains Mary, but I don't get John. He doesn't do anything impulsively."

"Mary's a virgin."

If Lauren and I had known each other for more than a couple of hours, this might not have stunned me. But we weren't on any kind of terms where this felt appropriate.

"Your face is the color of the napkins," she said. The cloth napkins were a Christmas-red color.

I was embarrassed, sure, but I couldn't let her get away with pointing it out. "You and Mary both, huh?" I shot back. "Two nuns living at a convent in Campbell?"

Lauren burst out laughing. "You're funny."

John came into the room. "What's so funny?"

"Nothing," Lauren said. "John, be a pal and get me another whiskey. I'm tired of wine."

"Yeah, okay." John pointed at me. "You?"

I shook my head and pointed at my wine glass, which held a half pour.

After John left, Lauren leaned back in her chair and said, "It's only Mary who won't do anything until she's married."

Even though I knew it was the playful banter of a twenty-three-year-old girl who'd had a bit of alcohol, it was unnerving. I lifted the napkin. "I guess I'm this color again."

"You are. I'm being so polite, you have no idea."

"I'm sure I don't." I took my napkin and held it out like a matador facing a standing bull.

She fell back and laughed.

"So Mary's name fits her," I said. "And you're the opposite of her, so the name Lauren must mean eas—"

"Watch it!" Lauren took her napkin and threw it at me.

John returned with Lauren's drink. "Hey, don't assault our guests."

"He deserves it," Lauren said.

"I do."

Mary came in carrying two plates with cheesecake. "How's it going in here? You guys getting along?" I couldn't help looking at her differently. There was a certain glow, like pregnant women have, and her voice carried a sweetness to it that I hadn't caught before.

"Well, Lauren is throwing things at Steve, but other than that, it's going fine."

"He started it," Lauren said.

Mary set a large piece of cheesecake in front of me and then handed Lauren hers. "Can I trust you not to jab anyone with this fork?" she said to Lauren.

Lauren shook her head. "No."

"I promise to be better," I said. "It's just—um, let's say, my Latin is a little rusty."

"Ha," Lauren said. "Besides, it's French."

"My French is even worse," I said.

"What were you guys talking about?" John asked.

Lauren said, "Nothing." She looked over at Mary. "Where's the ring? Do you have one yet?"

"I'm having it resized. It was a little big. I was really hoping to get it back today, but it wasn't ready yet."

"How did you propose?" I asked John.

John and Mary glanced at each other and laughed. "Actually, it sort of just happened," John said.

"Huh?" I said. "How's that?"

Mary told the story. They were at a restaurant when someone proposed. A man had gotten down on a knee, and the whole restaurant froze while the man asked her. The woman accepted and everyone in the restaurant clapped. John then said something about how proposing in public is dangerous unless you've already discussed it, which means it's not really a proposal, just a formality. He told Mary that he would have gone about it differently, privately, as a surprise. So Mary said, are you proposing to propose? She said she didn't need an event for their proposal and so they got engaged.

"I guess a proposal to propose is a proposal," I said.

I looked at Lauren and she was surreptitiously doing the imaginary reeling gesture again. I smiled and lightly shook my head at her.

We chatted a bit more. Lauren left not long after. I stayed a few minutes later, until around nine thirty, and went home, surprised at how the evening had turned out. I was intrigued by Lauren, who was dangerous. But I was also intrigued by Mary—even more dangerous.

Chapter Six

August 1999

JOHN AND I INTERACTED LESS FREQUENTLY over time. What started as a monthly meet-up at Moe's Way (always coordinated with Mary's schedule at SGF) eventually stretched to every two to three months. And though we still talked on the phone regularly, the calls occurred more sparingly. It wasn't a great surprise that this happened—we weren't working together, plus he was spending more time with Mary, which was natural. When we did speak or get together, the friendship felt no less distant—we were still good friends and easily picked up where we had left off. Admittedly, he started to annoy me as it got closer to the wedding. The drama around wedding plans wasn't something I had much interest in.

On a Wednesday in late August, John called me up at the office. It was ten to eight in the morning, and it was unusual because he knew I didn't normally arrive before eight thirty. He fumbled with his words for a few seconds before I interrupted. I told him that I needed to leave for a meeting in a few minutes. He got straight to the point: Did I want to go out with him, Mary, and Lauren on Friday night to celebrate Mary's new job?

"Don't feel obligated to go," he said before I could answer.

"Why wouldn't I go?"

"I mean, you don't have to if you don't want to since Lauren will be there. I know she can be a bit much to handle."

After that one dinner where John and Mary announced they were engaged, I had seen Lauren four or five times, mostly at SGF. Once, John threw a birthday party for Mary at his townhouse, and I spent a half hour alone with Lauren outside on the small back patio. Though we weren't friends, Lauren and I did have this strange connection. Being the best friends of John and Mary, we were the ones who saw the two of them up close.

"It's not like a date, right?" I said.

"No, no. Of course not. Mary asked me to invite you so Lauren wouldn't feel bad about herself."

"Lauren? Feel bad about herself?"

"I know. But apparently she's been upset lately because her ex-boyfriend has been bothering her again."

"Sure, I'll go," I said.

"Great," he said. He gave me the time and place to meet.

I hung up, gathered a notebook, and headed for the conference rooms, which were no small distance away in the interior of the building. As I got close to the room, one of the people who should have been part of the meeting was heading in the opposite direction. "Is the meeting canceled?" I asked him.

"No, it got changed at the last minute. I guess Rebecca sent out an email about it, but I must have missed it. I think they still want you there."

I hadn't seen an email from Rebecca, who was my boss. The meeting was supposed to be about repurposing servers used for Y2K end-to-end testing. Now I didn't know what it was about.

The conference rooms were windowless. Normally if a door was closed, I'd open it a crack to see if the last meeting hadn't finished. But it was eight o'clock in the morning, so I fully opened the door without hesitation and was wholly unprepared for who was actually there.

Dumbstruck is probably the exact word to describe my reaction. In fact, Rebecca said, "Good morning," to me twice because I stood there, with the door still open, too confused—too scared—to speak or move. My mind was rushing to make sense of it all. What was going on here?

Rebecca was on the opposite side of the table from the door where I was standing. To her left was Megan Stanton.

The nearest chair to me was empty, and in the next seat, a woman was gazing at me eerily. If it weren't for her heterochromatic eyes, it would have taken me a lot longer to recognize her—I had successfully avoided running into her for the last four years (I never went to the cafeteria before twelve thirty). What I saw was a blond woman who reminded me of a heavier, though still thin, Tiffany Popiel who couldn't possibly have been Tiffany Popiel because there was no reason for me to be in a meeting with her. But those eyes made it undeniable!

At the far end of the table was Jake Fitzgerald. I was glad to see F. Jake, and I felt a little relieved—unless he was a witness for the prosecution. He was no longer part of the Y2K group. He now worked at one of the business units, consumer services. He grinned and lifted his Styrofoam cup in a cheerful gesture. "Good morning, Mr. Galanos."

"Am I in the right meeting?" I asked, my mouth suddenly dry.

"Yes," Rebecca said. "Have a seat, Steve."

"Okay," I said, closing the door. "What's this all about?"

"This is Tiffany Popiel from product marketing," Rebecca said.

"We know each other," Tiffany said, and said it in such a disinterested way that it must have come across as strange to the others.

"Yeah," I said, and sat down in the chair closest to me without making eye contact with anyone except Rebecca.

Rebecca explained the reason we were there. It was about a license dispute with one of our software vendors, Unity Software. I knew the dispute well—a license that we did not renew even though we continued to use it. It had been on a system that was being eliminated, and when we signed the last agreement, for several hundred thousand dollars, we got an email from the Unity salesman saying that we could use it for a "reasonable extended period" if our migration took longer. Which, of course, it did. It was an old piece of software anyway that was not Y2K compliant. It took an extra three months to fully shut off that system after the end date of the contract. A three-month delay at the phone company was totally "reasonable."

So we didn't pay any more when a new Unity sales rep showed up asking for more money.

"Our legal department agreed that we didn't need to pay it," I said.

"Yes," Rebecca said, "but . . ." She pointed a hand at Tiffany.

"Early next year," Tiffany said, "we are relaunching our digital subscriber line under the name Blaze."

"And guess who owns the trademark to the name," F. Jake said.

"Unity?" I said.

"Yep. Unity will let us use the name, but only if we pay what they think we owe them," F. Jake said.

"It's a hundred and sixty thousand dollars," I said.

"I know," F. Jake said.

"For legacy software that no one uses anymore and that we already overpaid for. No way we give them another penny."

"I appreciate your view of this, Steve," Rebecca said. "But at this point this isn't really about paying them for their software."

Megan asked, "Is this name really worth a hundred and sixty thousand dollars?"

Tiffany nodded. "We've already created marketing materials around Blaze and—"

"Even a TV ad," F. Jake cut in. "And it's with a famous actor—I can't say who."

"Yeah, so changing the name now would delay the product launch by several months," Tiffany finished.

I wanted to ask Tiffany why they didn't check to see if someone else was using the name before running with it, but I wasn't about to antagonize her.

"And we don't want to delay this at all. DSL is going to be huge for us," F. Jake said.

This whole scene was surreal and the circumstances were extremely unusual. I laughed. I couldn't help myself—I had spent hours with a lawyer, determining that we didn't have to pay and then helping the lawyer draft a response to their letter accusing us of breach and then a second letter . . . and now this.

"What's so funny?" Rebecca asked.

"Nothing. It's just—this is completely out of left field." I meant all of it, the situation with Unity and being in a meeting with Tiffany and Megan. Even F. Jake—talking with him about something other than Y2K remediation was strange to me.

Another person walked into the room, a man with dark brown hair perfectly combed and wearing a crisp white shirt and olive-green slacks. "Sorry I'm a little late," he said.

He looked at me and then introduced himself. "I'm Mike Cobb, director of product marketing." I told him my name and shook hands with him. F. Jake flashed a jaunty wave from his end of the table. Mike Cobb already knew Rebecca. Megan introduced herself.

"Are we all up to speed?" Mike Cobb asked.

"Mostly," Rebecca said.

"Good. So we can just pay Unity and move on?" He had maneuvered himself to the front of the room, remained standing, with his hands on the back of a chair.

"Who's paying it?" I asked.

"That's what I wanted to talk about next," Rebecca said.

Megan shook her head. "If it's an invoice to IT service delivery, IT service delivery has to pay it. Period."

"It's not in the budget," I said.

Rebecca nodded. "I know, but is there another choice?"

"No," Megan said. "I mean, marketing could do a budget transfer, but corporate isn't going to approve that. Not for that amount."

"So we're stuck holding the bag," I said.

"I wish we could do something to help," Mike Cobb said. His brooding grimace came across as insincere.

"I'll need to confirm with Mr. Clifton on this," Rebecca said. "He's going to have to approve this."

"Sounds good. And if you need me to talk to him, just let me know," he said. "I know Rex pretty well. We go to the same gym."

The meeting ended there and I immediately got up to leave. Rebecca asked me to stay behind. F. Jake patted me on the back as he walked by. "Let's do lunch soon," he said.

I nodded and then sat back down, waiting awkwardly for Megan and Tiffany to gather their things—especially Megan, who lifted a black tote bag and started rearranging things. Several files and her laptop were sitting on the table. I didn't want to be caught staring, so I turned my attention to a painting on the wall. Someone had once told me that the artwork around the office was worth a lot of money. I didn't know if this was one of those expensive pieces. It was a childlike painting with bursting asterisks and colorful smudges surrounding a dancing bear or mouse or—

"Your anniversary just passed, and I wanted to discuss your review," Rebecca said once the door closed.

I blinked a few times and then said, "I can't believe we're going to pay Unity."

"Look, I know you like doing things the right way, but in this case, there isn't much we can do. If we fight it, it goes all the way to the top and we end up paying it anyway."

I could have vented some more, but the deep creases around her frown said it all. She wasn't interested in talking about it anymore. "I'm sure you're right," I sighed.

"So about your review . . . I particularly want to talk to you about your goals, Steve. As you know, this company has a strong interest in career development."

My seventh anniversary hadn't passed me by unnoticed. Plainly my job was unfulfilling. Finding a new job was possible, but I didn't think much would really change except maybe the cube walls would be a different shade of gray-taupe. Perhaps it was the three cups of coffee that I'd had that morning, or perhaps it was the meeting we'd just had, like a bad Fellini dream sequence warping my mind. Or maybe after talking to John that morning, I felt abandoned in a pit of "the Old Economy." Regardless, a wave of dangerous casual indifference swelled in me, daring me to be careless.

"Should I be candid or do you want the standard 'I want to do my current job well and have progressively more responsibility'?"

She let out an apprehensive chuckle. "Be candid, of course.

Please."

I knew she didn't mean it. But she wasn't about to say otherwise. So after a long second of contemplating, I said, "I basically hate my job. Don't get me wrong. I don't have an issue working for you. I'm just tired of the same old thing every day."

"Well, maybe you need a change. Maybe you should consider working in a different department."

"Like what?"

"I don't know. What are you interested in?"

I shrugged. That was part of the problem. I had no desire to be a cog anywhere in this large machine or any other machine. "I don't know. I just don't feel like my work is important."

"If it weren't for us, if we didn't do our jobs, we wouldn't have functioning data centers. And without functioning data centers, no one would be talking on the phone."

A sarcastic laugh urged to get out—to think that I was partially responsible for the communications network in this state was absurd. I said, "Our work is forgotten almost as soon as it's completed. It evaporates. I mean, look at today—I wasted my time on this Unity thing."

"Not everything we do turns out to be fruitful. But your efforts are always appreciated."

I gave a slight shrug.

"What about doing something completely different that might be more fulfilling? Sometimes a hobby can turn into a career. What do you like to do outside of work?"

"Watch sports. Bet on games."

"That's it? You don't have any other hobbies? Musical

instrument? Scuba diving?"

I shook my head. "I live in an apartment. My neighbors generally frown on extra noise. As for scuba diving, I'm claustrophobic."

"Do you have a dream job?"

"Teacher."

"Really?" she said, looking a bit surprised. She quickly added, "Why not pursue that?"

My laugh wasn't intended to insult her, but it had that effect. She fell back in her seat with a sulking expression. How was I supposed to get into teaching at that point in my life? I'd have to go back to school and make very little money for a long while. "I'm almost thirty-five years old. It's too late for me," I explained. "Far too late."

"It's never too late."

"Too many sacrifices," I said.

"Sometimes you have to make sacrifices to get somewhere."

I nodded. "So are you going to fire me now?"

"No, of course not. We all feel like you do about our jobs from time to time. And I can see why you'd feel like that right now."

Here is where I should have stopped, but I had let go too much line, too much of that side of me that is the opposite of my natural reticence, and I couldn't reel it back in. The conversation stayed on this general topic of career happiness and ended up with me generalizing: "Given the choice, which is what married women have, I'd stay home, raise the kids, and then have free time . . . lots of free time once the kids are in school."

Rebecca had two children and her husband was a lawyer.

"Free time to gamble on sports?" she shot back.

I spurted out a laugh. "Sure. Why not?"

On Friday night, I drove to Campbell, to an open-air shopping center with several restaurants and retail shops. As I headed for the door of Redrock Grill and Bar, where I was meeting Mary, Lauren, and John, I heard my name called. It was John walking toward me at a brisk pace, a large grin on his face.

He grabbed my outstretched hand to shake. He held on with such possessive energy that I wasn't sure when he was going to let go. "Hey, it's great to see you!" he said.

"Yeah, you too." I was a bit surprised because my original impression was that he didn't want me at dinner that night. "You seem pretty excited."

"I'm in a good mood." He patted me on the back as we headed for the door. "The lock-up agreement ended today. I can sell my shares on Monday."

I had seen the stock price of the company where John worked. It had exploded over the last two months, tripling from its initial public offering. "That's awesome!" I said, trying not to sound inauthentic. Weighing on my heart was a mixed but mostly bitter feeling. Sure, I was glad for him—and Mary, too, as the two were set to be married in six weeks. But a slurry of jealousy, inadequacy, and abandonment blocked my best regards for his overweight luck.

As we walked toward the restaurant, I realized that we were both wearing the same clothes. Roughly. Blue jeans and a light blue dress shirt, though my button-up had thin white stripes and his carried a brand icon. He wore his shirt untucked, which I did not (Friday dress code at the phone company was casual but never sloppy). I quickly rolled up my sleeves before going inside the restaurant.

"Yeah, thank God for that lock-up agreement," he said as we went inside.

When the company had gone public, those who had shares in the stock options had been barred from selling for six months.

"Oh yeah? Why?"

John held up a finger to me and approached the maître d'. The plan was to meet Mary and Lauren at the bar, have a drink, and then eat at the restaurant at seven o'clock. The bar was through the restaurant, a few steps higher than the main floor. I spotted Mary and Lauren sitting at a counter-height table.

As we headed toward the bar, John said, "If that lock-up didn't exist, I would have sold as soon as I could."

Mary got off the tall chair when we reached the table. She was wearing a flowy white top, off the shoulder, and dark blue jeans. Her black hair brushed against her bare shoulders, and her bright red lipstick accentuated the fullness of her lips. I had seen Mary plenty of times, but not like this, made up for a night out on the town. She gave John a light kiss and greeted me with a warm smile and a hug.

"Congratulations on your new job," I said to her.

Lauren greeted us with an aloof smile. She remained seated as John went over and lightly embraced her, placing his arm over her shoulders for a second. "Hello," she said.

Swede 11, in her black mock-neck tank top and long blond curls, aroused in me that defensive mechanism aimed at hiding nervousness.

I had seen Lauren enough times to not have this reaction. Sticking out my hand stiffly, I said, "Hi, I'm Steve. It's nice to meet you."

I was being childish, of course, but it stumped her for a long second, as if she thought it might be true. Lauren slapped my hand away. "Shut up."

I felt like I was seventeen, in my high school government class sitting next to the head cheerleader. With a drink in me, I'd get over it.

As we sat down, John said, "Everything tonight is on me. So please enjoy!"

"Thanks," I said.

Lauren's expression remained flat, as if she hadn't expected otherwise.

After a waiter took our drink order, Mary said, "You guys just missed it."

"Missed what?" John asked.

"Lauren scared the heck out of a guy."

We all stared at Lauren, waiting for an explanation. Lauren laughed coolly and stirred the red straw in her Long Island iced tea. "Just having a little fun."

While Mary was in the restroom, Lauren had spotted a man sitting at the bar eyeing her. He kept turning to look at her, and she could tell he was trying to muster enough courage to come over. After she caught him slipping his wedding ring into his pocket, Lauren signaled the waiter and ordered the man a drink, adding, "But tell him it's from his wife." Mary came back then, and Lauren told her what she had done. They watched as the man got his drink and nervously searched around. He snapped his fingers at the bartender, who listened for a second before shaking his head.

"The guy ran out of here so fast," Mary said. "Lauren waved at him as he left." She reenacted the gesture, a dainty cupping of her hand.

"Yeah, he looked a little freaked out," Lauren said. She placed her hand on John's arm. "There's going to be a rum and Coke on your tab."

When John and I got our drinks, we toasted to Mary and her new career. As we clinked glasses, I glanced at Lauren, whose forced smirk reflected my excitement over John's fortunes.

"And here's to you, sweetheart," Mary said to John.

"Oh, come on," John said. "This is your night."

"For what?" Lauren said.

"Lock-up ended today at John's company," she said. "He can sell his shares anytime now."

It struck me that the celebration tonight was not really for Mary's new job. It was for John—at least that's what he was celebrating. He didn't care about Mary's job. The money it would bring was irrelevant to him.

We all clinked glasses.

"So how much did you make?" Lauren asked. From anyone else, it might have come across as an inappropriate question. But Lauren had this nosy indifference. If someone refused to answer her, she'd shrug and make it seem as if she hadn't even really cared to know in the first place.

"More than I deserve," John said. The modest response was a cover. He really wanted to say, and after taking a drink of his beer, he did. "Over two million. Though I can't sell all of that quite yet."

Though I had never asked him, that was a bit more than I had calculated. To hear it confirmed out loud caused me to shrink inside a little more.

Before we left for our table in the restaurant, John visited the restroom. While he was gone, Lauren peppered Mary with questions about her new job.

"I don't understand why you took this job," Lauren said. "I mean, John's got all this money now."

"You know I've always wanted to do this."

"He's not making you sign a prenup, is he?"

Mary shook her head indignantly. "No, of course not."

"Then I don't get it. I mean, who cares about all that career stuff anyway?"

"I didn't get my marketing degree for nothing. I want to see what I could do out there," Mary answered.

"If you gave me the choice not to work, I'd ditch the job in a heartbeat."

"And what would you do? Go shopping every day?" Mary said.

Lauren smiled. "Sure, why not?"

Mary shook her head. "Well, I'm only doing this until I'm ready to have children."

Lauren shrugged. "I guess it doesn't matter, then. You'll be pregnant in no time."

"That's not the plan," Mary said in a firm tone.

"Unplanned happens. Even still, I mean, what's the point you're trying to prove? It's not like you're a doctor saving lives or something important."

Mary became quiet.

There was a couple hovering around, sort of annoyingly, waiting for a table to become available at the bar. Standing up, I said, "It's five to six. Let's head over and tell them we're ready for our table."

Dinner did not lack conversation; however, it did lack some diversity. Much of the talk revolved around the upcoming wedding and honeymoon. Mostly Mary talked—maybe this was her way of needling Lauren: *I'm getting married and you're not.* Or perhaps because Lauren and I were the only attendants, Mary felt she had some luxury of going into detail.

Whether it was a story about a slighted second or third cousin once removed who was not invited or the final decisions around flowers (including the pros and cons of adding a second bouquet for the bouquet toss), Lauren was as uninterested as I was. We regularly exchanged glances. For his part, John kept protesting this idea or that and getting overruled on any objection that had to do with reducing the elaborateness of the wedding.

I politely asked questions as if I were listening intently, and for Mary's sake I hid my boredom. After Lauren finished her second drink, her sarcastic comments became more caustic, though who really knows if the alcohol had anything to do with it—"It's too late to change that, so why are you agonizing over it?" After one too many, Mary exclaimed, "I hope you don't run into any trouble whenever you decide to get married, Lauren." Luckily the waitress showed up just then and asked if we wanted dessert. We all declined.

An argument broke out outside the restaurant over whether any one of us was sober enough to drive to downtown Campbell. It was less than a mile away. I suggested walking there, but that was met with hostility from both Lauren and John, who insisted that he was under the legal limit. Mary pointed to a couple of bars nearby that they could walk to.

John called out to Lauren, who had started for the parking lot. After debating with Mary for a few more seconds, John gave chase, beckoning Lauren to come back.

The next place we went to ended up being another bar inside of a restaurant, though this place had its own door and own name, the Rinse. Mary said they made special martinis there. I didn't care for a martini but it was her night, and I wasn't going to argue. We sat at the bar, Mary, John, Lauren, and I in a row, which was impractical for a group conversation. We ordered our martinis.

Mary asked for an appletini, which I had never heard of. Lauren ordered a Grey Goose dirty martini. I asked her why she wasn't getting an appletini like Mary. "Those things will be popular with suburban moms one day," she said to me, and then added with a snicker, "Mary will be joining them very soon."

Mary said, "You guys are boring," to John and me—we had ordered plain vodka martinis. And I suppose our drinks did look dull against her bright green one. I took a sip of Mary's appletini to satisfy my curiosity and have never tasted one since.

Sitting next to each other at the bar, Lauren and I started having a good time together. I didn't know whether it was the alcohol or a camaraderie—we being the flops who didn't have two million dollars, weren't starting a new job or getting married. She turned to me and said, "I can't wait for the wedding to be over. How about you?"

I leaned toward her ear, and in a mocking voice, I said, "Should we do little plants as wedding favors or candles?"

She laughed. "Jordan almonds, I think." And each time we started on something together, John nudged in. "What's so funny?" he'd ask.

Finishing the last sips of our martinis, I told Lauren about my awkward reunion earlier in the week with Tiffany Popiel and Megan Stanton, whom I only referred to as my ex-girlfriends. I blame the alcohol for greasing the skids, yet this was my warped way of impressing her—showing that I wasn't a sad, lonely bachelor. Lauren cracked up and said, "Sorry, I don't mean to laugh. You poor thing."

John asked, "What happened?"

Mary seemed a little annoyed, being on the far left and mostly out of the conversation. "Let's go to Bendz."

"Who's Ben?" I asked.

Lauren laughed. "Bendz with a 'dz' at the end. It's a lounge in downtown Campbell."

"How are we getting there?" I asked.

"We'll get a cab," Mary said.

As we were leaving, John said, "What were you talking about?"

"Steve got ambushed at a meeting by two ex-girlfriends."

"Not exactly ambushed," I said.

"What girlfriends?" John asked.

I didn't answer him. We left the bar and slalomed our way through the small lobby. There was a growing crowd of people hanging outside, too, waiting to have dinner at the restaurant.

The air outside was perfectly warm, the last bit of light slowly withdrawing from the sky.

Mary told John to call a cab.

"I left my phone in the car. The battery was dead."

I didn't own a cellphone—I really didn't see the point since there was no one who urgently needed to get ahold of me.

"There's a payphone by the theater," Mary said.

As we headed toward the movie theater, John said, "I don't recall you having a girlfriend at work."

"I never told you about them because it never became too serious."

The four of us contemplated for a minute whether we should see a movie, which quickly veered into a discussion about how much candy and alcohol we could actually sneak into the theater. But when we got there, no one really wanted to see a movie, so John went over to the payphone and called us a cab.

Lauren and Mary wandered over to a metal bench that faced the parking lot. They sat down. I remained near them, standing behind the bench, waiting for John.

John came over a half minute later and told us the taxi would be there in five minutes.

"Do I know them?" John asked me.

"Who?"

"Your girlfriends."

I lied and told him no. He knew Megan, though not Tiffany.

"Maybe I did know them," he said. "What's their names?"

"No, you wouldn't know them. One's in marketing."

"I knew people in marketing."

"Who?"

"Swede 8!" he said.

Of course I was stunned that he mentioned "Swedes" in front of other people. Especially these two. But I also wanted to correct him once and for all. Swede 8 was in corporate communications, not marketing!

"Swede 8?" Mary said, turning around.

John stumbled with a series of *um's*, and I worried that he might try to explain. I couldn't have been too drunk after all, because I quickly bailed him out. "Yeah, we worked with this Swedish girl who claimed she was seventh runner-up in a beauty pageant in Sweden. So we gave her this nickname."

"That's not nice of you guys," Mary said. "Still, she must have been really pretty to have gotten that far."

"She was all right," I said, and that might have been the biggest lie of all about Swede 8.

Lauren said, "Why wouldn't you guys call her Swede 7?"

John and I exchanged a glance—Joanna being Swede 7—and if I hadn't been horrified that we were discussing Swedes with Swede 11 and Mary, I would have burst out laughing. "Well, she was the seventh runner-up. The runner-up is second place," I said.

"Yeah," John said. "Like the first floor in Europe is really the second floor here."

I looked at John askance. We were already free from his blunder. There was no need to overexplain, which always hints that something is amiss.

"No, that's not true," Mary said. "Not in Sweden."

"How do you know that?" John asked, skepticism in his tone.

"Sure, you're always right, honey." Mary sat back against the bench and crossed her arms.

This caused Lauren's face to turn up, and her eyes brightened.

"I didn't say I was right. I just asked how you know that."

"Because I've been to Sweden," Mary said, staring out into the parking lot.

"You have? When?"

"When I was in high school."

I traded glances with Lauren. She was really enjoying this. And at least we were off discussing the naming and numbering of attractive women as Swedes.

"I thought you said you hadn't been to Europe," John continued with Mary. "When we were talking about where to go on our honeymoon."

Mary turned to face John. "No, I never said that."

"Yeah, you did. You said that we should go there instead of Hawaii because neither of us had been there."

"I think you two need to date more before you get married," Lauren said.

Mary ignored Lauren's comment. "I meant neither of us had been to the places in Europe where everyone goes. France, Italy, Germany, England."

"What about Greece?" I said.

"Yeah, Greece, too. Definitely," Mary said.

"How did you end up going to Sweden? Seems odd," John said.

Mary explained that their neighbors the Dahlströms moved back to Sweden when she was in high school. "They invited us to visit them, so we went in the summer between my junior and senior year. It was a really fun trip."

On Mary's instructions, the cab stopped suddenly, and we all got out. We weren't at Bendz. We were standing near railroad tracks, and the closest building was about a block away, beyond the crossing gates. John asked why we had gotten out there.

"That street is one way, and it would've taken another five minutes to go all the way around to get to Bendz."

Mary noticed John's unsatisfied look, so she added, "That taxi really smelled. Didn't it smell to you?"

John shook his head, I shrugged, and Lauren said, "No worse than any other cab I've been in."

Mary waved us off and started quickly down the sidewalk. John walked to keep up with her while Lauren and I followed at our own pace.

After crossing the train tracks, we approached an older-looking building. A loud bass emanated from there, and I said to Lauren, "Do I need my earplugs for this place?"

"That's not where we're going," she said. "You're such an old man, though."

"Hey!" I nudged her gently in the ribs with my elbow.

She laughed and we stared at each other for a second, long enough to pass an understanding between us—that we were on our own now, not simply attached as friends to John and Mary.

Bendz, housed in an old brick building, had a large open space between the bar and the lounge. The lounge appeared to be completely occupied by people. The middle space was quite full, too, twentysomethings standing and drinking and talking. It was loud in there, but there wasn't any music yet, so Mary didn't have to yell when she told us she was going to find us a place to sit.

I almost asked if there was a college nearby, but I was afraid Lauren would label me old again. Besides, it was August, so that didn't make sense anyway.

Mary did her magic and waved us over. She had managed to corral some furniture and created a snug space for us, two leather benches in an L shape with a small table in the middle.

The waitress came by, and we ordered drinks. I went for a beer here because the martini had left me reeling a little bit.

Mary ordered a glass of wine. John went for a whiskey and soda. Lauren asked for a mojito.

We mostly watched and talked about the people standing around. There were more men than women. After we finished our drinks, Lauren got up and grabbed me by the hand.

"Come and buy me a drink," Lauren said. "I really want another mojito." She pulled me off the couch and through the crowd and to the bar. We got drinks—both mojitos. We stayed at the bar for a long while, drinking and making fun of the crowd.

At one point, Lauren brought up her ex-boyfriend, who she said was stalking her. By this time, I was not feeling myself anymore. I hadn't had that much to drink in a long time—not since my sophomore year of college.

She explained that this ex-boyfriend of hers was constantly calling her at home and work and hanging up the phone. I must have sounded unimpressed, because then she said that he'd show up to her work and leave notes and flowers on her car.

"Sounds scary," I said, using a sincere tone, though I really didn't know how serious this was.

"I'm very close to getting a restraining order," she said.

"Is he capable of violence?"

"Once he threatened to drag me by the hair. So what do you think?"

Back with Mary and John, Lauren started talking about the next place to go to. I told them that I was out. And after a few pleas from Mary, and even some from Lauren, which seemed sincere, I bowed out. It was going to be downhill for me going forward. So I left them to decide the next place. After visiting the restroom, I walked back to where we had started the night and sat in my car for about an hour. I felt good enough to drive, I just wasn't sure the law felt the same way.

Chapter Seven

September 1999

SINCE THE DAY I MET HER, I had never been alone with Mary. We were always around John, and usually Lauren, too. But there was one occasion where it was only Mary and me, and on that day, I fell in love with her. I don't really mean that in the normal sense of that phrase. It wasn't like I'd have done anything to win her favor or she was constantly on my mind—though I thought about her perhaps more than I'd have cared to admit at the time. Sure, if John hadn't been in the picture, and given the chance, I would have asked her out—I'd even joked about it with John, that if he had actually gotten farther into SGF that night and had convinced Lauren to date him, Mary and I might have ended up together.

The circumstances of our meeting were totally unnecessary and somewhat ridiculous given that we could have simply had a conversation over the phone. It had to do with John's bachelor party. I wanted Mary's blessing for my plan.

So on that day, a perfectly warm day in early September, I met Mary at a popular sandwich shop a few miles north from where she lived.

Mary had an emerging beauty—she was strikingly different from Lauren, whose figure and face and unaffected entitlement could hardly be matched. Mary's beauty grew on me, those little things missed or overlooked that then tingled my heart when I finally noticed them. Only when you spend time with someone do these blossom, whether a personality trait or a physical feature like her sneeze, which sounded as if someone were tickling a baby.

I asked Mary to meet me, secretly, for lunch—*Don't tell John or Lauren!* This was about a month before the wedding. When I started planning for the bachelor party, I found that John didn't have any friends in California. I would have reached out to his friends from Ohio, but he wasn't inviting any of them to the wedding. So I planned a different kind of bachelor party, one that was better off with Mary's explicit consent, especially given my somewhat limited knowledge of her. Like her temper, which according to John had amassed from her heritage—a circuitous route from the Spanish Canary Islands, down to Argentina, and landing in Puerto Rico before coming to America.

The bachelor party I had planned was, in fact, nothing wild. We weren't twenty-two-year-old frat boys, after all—though plenty our age took excursions to Vegas and Cabo. Since it was just going to be John and me, my plan was a little different. I thought it was best to get Mary's approval, so I used that as a good excuse to see her in person and have lunch.

"Are you secretly in love with me?" she said in my ear after we had stumbled into a hug.

This threw me for a second, because we had never teased each other like that. It wasn't part of our relationship. "Is it that obvious?" was all I could come up with.

She slapped me lightly on the shoulder and we talked about what to order for lunch. When we sat down, I told her that I wanted to discuss the bachelor party, and I didn't want John to know that we were meeting.

"What are you planning to do?" she asked. Her dark eyes narrowed ever so slightly, and given John's stories about their arguments, I became faintly nervous.

"Well, you see, um, I'm hoping to disrupt your bachelorette party."

She laughed. "What do you mean by that?"

"Just mess around with it a bit, but I haven't figured it all out yet," I said. I gave her a vague outline. "And I do want you to be surprised, too."

"I can't help you with any details, even if I wanted to. Lauren is planning it all, and she hasn't told me a thing."

I assured her that it wouldn't be a problem and that I was bringing John into it the next day. "I'm not telling him that I spoke to you. That would ruin the fun of it." Though I was certain I'd have to convince him of it. "I just wanted to make sure you weren't going to be upset, because that would be awful all around."

"No, of course not. I love the idea. Can't wait to see what happens." She smiled, and her sweet dimples emerged.

"Though," she said, more seriously, "Lauren might get mad at you. Really mad at you."

I shrugged. "I can live with that. She'll never know it was us—as long as *you* don't tell her."

She motioned with her fingers, zipping her lips.

We talked about the wedding. She was both excited and nervous. "I've been planning this day since I was eight years old."

"Eight? Seriously?"

"Yeah, every girl dreams of a fantastic wedding. It's supposed to be the greatest day of your life."

John didn't feel the same way. He wanted to be done with it. He had told me he wished they could just go to the courthouse and get it over with. "The only way to get away with that," he had told me, "is if you're marrying someone who's been divorced."

After eating lunch, Mary suggested we go miniature golfing. "Mini golf?" I said, letting out a small laugh. "Sure, let's go!" I added with sarcasm.

"I'm serious." She pointed and said there was a course two blocks down the street. "I know it's silly, but sometimes I like to do something that reminds me of when I was younger. Don't you?"

"Yeah . . ." It was certainly charming, quite contrary to the punctilious view of Mary that had been impressed on me. Then again, it was an innocent kids' game of mini golf, out in the open. There was no reason, really, to think anything salacious about it. Still, what would John think? What would he—

"It'll be our little secret," she said without my prompting. Perhaps it was the torn look that must have lingered on my face. "Just like the bachelorette thing."

Without my reply, she pointed toward the restroom. "I'll be right back."

The sun felt good coming out of the sandwich shop, which was air-conditioned for a much hotter day. After a minute—waiting for Mary to come out—I positioned myself in the long shade of a cypress tree.

The girl who had been planning her wedding since age eight now wanted to be eight again—was she having second thoughts? I didn't think so. Reaching the culmination of a longtime fantasy must have hit her, that she was about to be thrust permanently into adulthood and the balance of her life.

I can't deny a thrill surged through me, imagining the two of us suspended together, alone, in secret—even if it was to play a child's game. Better yet, really. Quite possibly it would be one of those days that would float forever, wistfully relived every so often in my mind.

Making a pact to keep this from John did elevate it to something . . . an illicit excursion? I didn't know. I imagined John, my best friend, finding out. It unnerved me. So as I waited for Mary to come out, I was determined to say farewell, make some excuse about how I'd forgotten some appointment. But when she walked outside, the giddy grin on her face struck me, and with a pang in my heart, I knew I couldn't deny her. Or rather, I couldn't deny myself the moment's possibilities.

The first hole was one of those where the cup is inside a small bowl atop a large molehill. Mary made me go first, and I hit it too softly, so that the yellow ball came back almost halfway. "As you can see, I haven't done this in a long time."

Mary smiled. She set her large purse on the orange plastic bench. "Why didn't you just leave it in the trunk?" I said. She waved me off as if it'd been a ridiculous question and rested her purple ball down on the corrugated mat. She struck the ball perfectly straight. It hit the cup, but a little too hard, so that it popped over. She gasped, then cheered as it stayed confined within the funnel and rolled gently into the cup.

"Wow!" I said as she yelled, "Hole in one!" running down the lane to retrieve her ball.

"Wait a second," I yelled after her. "Are you some kind of mini golf hustler? You said you haven't played in years."

She came back, a big smile on her face. "I haven't. Ten years or more. I swear."

Shaking my head, I set myself and hit my ball. Too hard. Too soft. Way too soft. "Are we keeping score?" I muttered. Finally I got it in.

We played behind a family with two boys—both under ten—and even with my struggles, we waited each time for them to finish their hole. The dad signaled; did we want to play ahead? Mary was looking at the two awkward teenagers playing behind us. I shook my head at the man and gave a wave of thanks.

After finishing the third hole, where the aim was to get it through the door of a red barn, opening and closing, we stood in the sun, waiting our turn. "I think it's time for this," Mary said, pulling out a bottle from her purse. Hard lemonade.

"Where did that come from?"

"At the sandwich place. I thought it'd make it a little more fun." She handed it to me.

"Sure," I said. "We might get thrown out of here, but . . ."

"It's only lemonade." She shrugged. "Besides, who's going to tell on us?"

"You surprise me sometimes." I opened the bottle, and we swapped sips of the drink.

She smiled demurely. "There's another one in my purse, so don't be shy."

Perhaps it was nothing to her, but the sharing of the bottle sent a thrill through me. Rather than taking both bottles out at the same time, she chose to share. My head swam wildly; I believed it was a sign of contrived intimacy.

Mary started talking about Y2K. She said she knew I'd worked on fixing Y2K at the phone company. I corrected her in that I wasn't directly involved in fixing it, not like John had been, but said I was certainly involved tangentially.

"Well, whatever, you certainly know a lot more about it than me. What do you think will happen?"

"What's John said to you about it?"

"He doesn't like talking about it."

"What do you mean?" I knew exactly what she meant. John had done the same with me, quickly steering conversations elsewhere whenever I brought it up. So I never brought it up. We would talk about the people he knew, but if I mentioned something specific about Y2K, he'd swiftly steer the conversation elsewhere.

"He told me he hates talking about it because he spent too much of his life working on it."

I had a theory about this. As with da Vinci and his *Saint Jerome,* John's perfectionism had gotten in the way of his completing the Y2K project. And so he'd quit. Maybe he even felt guilty. I don't know. But I didn't tell Mary this. "Are you worried about it?"

She shrugged, took a sip from the bottle. "A little. I don't know—I guess that's why I'm worried. I just don't know. What do you think might happen?"

This was September 1999. Earlier in the year, a poll of information technology workers had been taken, and the majority answered that something would go wrong, especially outside the United States. "Maybe a glitch here or there, but nothing that can't be quickly corrected. Nothing like those doomsday scenarios where the power shuts off as time zones enter the new millennium."

"So you think everything will be all right?"

"Yes."

I didn't go into details. I didn't explain "date windowing," the method most companies and governments employed to defuse the Y2K time bomb. The trick was to pick a pivot number, so that anything below the pivot got interpreted as the 2000s and anything above as the 1900s. Using a pivot of thirty, for example, twenty-nine would equal 2029 and thirty would equal 1930.

As time started running out, windowing became the preferred solution. A shortcut and lazy answer, if a necessary one. John left the phone company when date windowing started becoming a popular solution within Y2K circles. Since he tended toward perfectionism, windowing wasn't something he approved of. All of that talk about getting out before a certain point and new management at the phone company, I think it had mostly to do with John's seeing the writing on the wall. They would never finish in time doing it *his* way.

And then I said this to get my point across—and I specifically remember saying it because it felt like hyperbole at the time. "People aren't even going to remember Y2K five years from now."

She nodded and gave a solemn smile. "Thanks," she said. "I feel better."

Watching the kids ahead of us all at once laugh and bicker, I asked Mary if she wanted children. "Yes, of course," she said. "I want two. A boy and then a girl."

"That's specific."

"Will and Jane."

"That's very specific. John on board with all of this?"

"John only wants one. He said he liked being an only child. He doesn't think he missed out on anything."

"I'm an only child."

"He says he got extra attention from his parents because he was an only child. Do you think that?"

"I don't know about that," I said. "It's hard to say, but I always wanted a younger brother."

"Yeah. I have a brother and a sister, so I want at least two kids."

"When?"

"Let me get married first."

"I know, I know. But are you planning to wait awhile or . . ."

"A few years. I want to work for a little while. I'm so happy I got this job. Finally something where I can use my degree."

"Is it something you love doing?" I asked.

"I'm not sure. That's what I want to find out. I don't want to have regrets later, you know?"

"Yeah, I get it."

"Do you like your job or would you do something else?"

I told her about the conversation with my boss a few weeks earlier—though I left some of the more provocative parts out.

"You really want to be a teacher?" Mary said. "Like high school?"

"Yeah, high school or middle school. But . . ."

"But what? Just go back to school and do it."

"How? Move back in with my mom?"

"You can make it happen if you put your mind to it. You can do night classes."

Mary's confidence made me think that I could do it, and a burst of hope and excitement flowed through me. When I got home, I would look at enrolling in a program.

"Do you really bet on sports?" she asked me.

"Sometimes." Yes, *sometimes* was an understatement.

"Does John?"

"No, never on sports. But that's because he's only interested in teams he roots for. John and I do bet when we go golfing, though."

"Really? Do you want to bet me?"

"You want to play skins?"

"Skins? Is that like strip golfing?" She giggled, and in a coquettish gesture, she dropped her head slightly before resting her eyes back on me.

I felt my cheeks burning. "No, nothing like that," I said through a laugh. "It's where we bet, say, a dollar on each hole, but if we tie, the money goes to the next hole—doubled each time we tie, is how I like to play if it's just two people."

"You mean if we tie here, the next hole is worth two dollars, and if we tie again, the following hole is worth four?"

"Exactly."

"Okay. I'm game," she said as the family ahead of us moved on. "But let's do two dollars per hole instead of one."

This is how I learned never to bet against Mary. We tied on the first hole after we started betting. We tied the next hole too, but I swear she missed a putt on purpose. On the following hole, she missed two putts on purpose. She won the fourth hole, easily. "That's sixteen dollars for me."

I called her on it, and she shrugged. "It's not cheating, is it?"

"No, not technically, but . . ."

She smiled. "I wish we would have done this from the beginning."

By the time we were at the ninth hole, I was down twenty bucks. But more significantly, we were halfway through the course. It reminded me of the first time I went miniature golfing, when I was seven years old, for a friend's birthday party. It was four of us, and I was having such a great time. Then my friend's dad announced, "Hole nine. We're halfway." Suddenly I felt sad, that this was going to end. *How do I keep this going forever? How do I stop time?* I wondered. The fact that it was going to end ruined the rest of it—I couldn't enjoy it because I knew the fun would end soon.

Talking and laughing, feeling closer and more familiar as we played on, we had left the stiffness of a casual friendship far behind and had crossed into new territory, where everything was open between us. So after the windmill hole and before the crazy big loop that was causing a stir for the family ahead of us, I brought up Lauren.

"Why are you roommates with Lauren? She seems quite the opposite of you in many ways."

"You have no idea."

"You've been friends for a while, right?"

"Since high school." And she repeated what I already knew: that she befriended Lauren when Lauren came to their school after her father had died.

Mary looked away and then said, "I shouldn't be telling you this. So don't say anything, not even to John. I haven't even told him."

A tingle spread down my neck. Both the secrecy of it and that she hadn't told John. She was about to confide in me. "No, I won't. Promise."

She pointed a finger at me. "She'd kill me."

"I won't say anything," I said. I really wanted to know. "What is it?"

She took a drink of the hard lemonade, the second bottle, and then set it down on the bench.

"Lauren used to be fat."

"What?" I smiled, nearly laughed, thinking she wasn't serious. It was hard to imagine. But Mary kept the hard frown. "How fat?"

"She gained a lot of weight after her dad died. Probably forty pounds heavier than she is now."

"Wow."

"But even now she thinks she's fat. And if she's fat, what am I?" she said, looking down at herself. "Every time she says, 'I'm so fat,' it's her backhanded way of insulting me."

"Come on," I said, and even though she didn't fit society's version of perfection—Lauren did that—Mary had the curves of the woman I wanted to hold. "It sounds like she might even have a disorder."

She guffawed.

"What?"

She shook her head. "Nothing. I've already said more than I should have."

I really wanted to know. But I didn't push it, especially since I didn't want Mary to think I was obsessed with Lauren. Which I wasn't.

It felt like a date, and by the end I said, "All of this is our little secret, right?" I reaffirmed this not because I thought she'd tell John, but to cement this intimacy between us.

"Right," she said. "Just us."

"I'll see you at your bachelorette party," I said in the parking lot as we were about to part ways.

She smiled. "Looking forward to it."

We hugged, and I held her for an extra second. She reciprocated the long hug. She felt good in my arms, solid and true.

After we parted I almost yelled out, *John's a lucky guy,* across the parking lot. But only actors in sappy movies say such things, so I swallowed the sentiment even though I meant it. And I immediately missed her, and I wanted to see her again. But I knew the truth. The next time could never be better than that day—I would be a disappointment to her, especially since we would not be alone like this.

Chapter Eight

October 1999

THE DAY AFTER THE OFFER ON THE HOUSE WAS ACCEPTED, John called me up, asking if I'd meet him there after work to give my honest opinion of it. "Opinion?" I said. "Isn't it a little too late for that?" It was . . . sort of. He was sure that he could find some undisclosed defect with the house and break the contract. And if that didn't work, he was willing to forego his deposit.

The housing market in Silicon Valley in 1999 largely followed the dot-com boom. People in senior management like John weren't the only ones being granted stock options. Even office assistants were raking in a half million dollars or more from their options. Stories of vast riches reached every corner of the country—and the world—and people came. Add to that an ocean, a promiscuous bay, mountains, good weather, and a property tax code that sharply discourages old homeowners from moving, and you get a real estate supply-demand imbalance.

A period of absurdity took hold. People bid hundreds of thousands of dollars over the asking price on homes that were already largely overpriced. Sellers had to choose whom to give the house to among competing bids, and price didn't necessarily win out. Anxious buyers wrote personal biographies to sway the owners. The smart ones personalized them. If an old man loved his rose garden as if it were his own child, bidders promised to rear the gardens to perpetual blooms; if the seller adored dogs, bidders attached photos of themselves with an oblivious puppy on their lap.

Making my way down Highway 17 to meet John, the approaching mountains posed behind a reflecting haze. The range briefly morphed into formidable clouds low on a Midwestern horizon and then back into mountains. The sun, gasping its last for the day as I crept toward Los Gatos, kept a persistent glow behind the elongated peaks of one of the mountains embracing the town. A diaphanous green lingered over the closest inclines, which were covered by the craggy, woolly texture of trees and a few patches of dried pasture. The mountains farther away, an enigmatic purple, an impossible shadow at first, then the promise of something vaster just beyond. These were a plain backdrop for the native born, but for me they were a gift, a comforting boundary to an endlessly shifting world.

Following John's directions, I made a turn onto a street that led to Mistral Avenue, where John's new car—a gray Porsche Boxster—was parked streetside. He had traded in his baby-blue BMW for the Porsche just a few weeks earlier. John didn't understand why Mary got upset with him for buying a car two days before the wedding.

I parked behind him, and John's car door opened. The house we fronted could best be described as a bungalow.

Getting out of my car, I said, "Is this your house?" in an incredulous tone. The house must have been less than fifteen hundred square feet.

"This one?" He pointed with his thumb to the bungalow. "No, of course not. It's farther up the street. I would've had Mary arrested for forgery if she'd bought this house."

"Forgery?"

As we walked, John recounted how he and his newlywed wife went about buying the house . . . Mary did in fact have near carte blanche to find a house because it was virtually impossible to see properties only on the weekends. Houses sold as soon as they listed, especially in desirable neighborhoods. So it was left up to her to find their new home. John's main condition was that it had to be less than $1.3 million. After spending one day with the real estate agent, Mary asked him the absolute maximum they could afford. "It was a mistake to tell her because it's more desirable to grab something with an outstretched arm than close at hand," he said.

The agent took Mary to see the Los Gatos house two weeks and three failed bids later. At the time, John was on the opposite side of the planet in Bangalore, India. The company he worked for had shipped him there to evaluate the software development group of another company. The sole purpose of the acquisition was to gain their offshore staff. It seemed a hefty price to pay, $30 million, for a few hundred employees in

India, but the company where John worked was worth a billion dollars without ever having shown a black penny.

When Mary feverishly told him about the Los Gatos house, it was early morning in India on the day he was to head back home. The asking price was $1.3 million. She insisted that the bid had to be placed within an hour. He told her to make an offer with a 15 percent premium, as they had done on their last bids. She exasperatedly explained that they'd have no chance at that price and only a slim chance at $1.6 million—the absolute maximum price they could afford. Astonished by the whole thing and assured that it was the perfect house for them, barely awake and a little heady from several nights' short shrift, John agreed to the $1.6 million. "Since Mary could forge my signature better than me, she signed everything instead of faxing papers back and forth halfway around the world."

I laughed, understanding the forgery reference.

The houses here were spaced fairly close to each other. There were no driveways. "Is there an alleyway with the garage?"

"Yes, which I don't really like."

"Which house is it?" I asked.

We stopped in the middle of the street.

"I'm going to make you play the same game Mary made me play," he said.

"What game?"

When John had returned home from India, Mary greeted him with a glass of barely cold champagne. All she had told him over the phone was that the house was in a great neighborhood in Los Gatos and the house's statistics—square footage, beds, baths. When he asked her to describe the place, she refused, forcing him to wait until they drove over there.

"Guess which house."

I scanned this neighborhood of eclectic homes, looking for the one with a real estate sign. But no house in sight had one. That wasn't entirely surprising since it had sold in one day. I shrugged. "I don't know. Which one?"

"Come on," he insisted. He pivoted around and waved his arm. "It's one of these houses around us. Look around. Which one is worth one point six million dollars?"

None was, and I felt a little burdened, as if picking the wrong one might mean he'd rescind the offer. The scent from the nearby eucalyptus tree was vibrant, the rain from earlier in the day having aroused its leaves. I took in a deep, refreshing breath, thinking that the tree belonged there as much as me—and John. Without further protest, I perused each house.

I started from the right. The house was a Craftsman style certainly amenable to my tastes, but John and I had once had a disagreement over them. With their low-pitched roofs and wide fronts, he derided Craftsmans as "fatmans." I assumed he had mentioned this to Mary, so I crossed that off the list.

Directly in front of us was a white, Cape Cod–style house with its side-gabled roof and two dormers. A manicured lawn and showy perennials on each side of the pathway leading up to the house might have made this one a real contender. But there was no way this small, perfectly charming house was worth $1.6 million.

Farther down was a Spanish-style house with the typical stucco exterior, round arches, and red mission tile on the roof. Stucco and red tiles didn't mix well with my staid Midwestern tastes, and I guessed not John's, either. Though this one was a possibility.

Turning around, directly across the street was a two-story house with multiple gables that reminded me of a bad test in geometry. Each gable, including the one over the porch that jutted out from the house, had a decorative triangle trim, like an exposed roof truss. I might have thought it was this one, but ragged junipers blanketed much of the front landscape. I figured that even the most unaccomplished real estate agent would have forced the owner to clean that up.

That left two houses, and looking to the right—a one-story of indeterminate style with a stucco exterior painted a wet-concrete color—I blindly pointed to the far left and said, "That one . . . The yellow one with the sycamore in front."

"Yes," he said. "What do you think of it?"

For $1.6 million, any native Midwesterner like me expected acres of land and a waterfront mansion. So I said nothing, thinking that this must have been a joke—the real house was up on another street.

His eyebrows lifted as he waited for an answer, and I realized this was the house he was buying.

"It's . . . lovely."

He looked at me suspiciously. "Lovely?"

Lovely wasn't a word in my regular vocabulary—or any man's, really—but it conveyed the somewhat effeminate vibe. This refurbished farmhouse had some Victorian features—

ornate window trim, delicate scrollwork, and fine spindles around the porch. It was the first compliment that popped into my mind, as I was still rather shocked he had paid so much for it. "Um . . . yeah, it's nice."

"I'm taking back the offer."

"No, it's really nice," I said with more enthusiasm, not wanting to be blamed for John's decision. I imagined him in a conversation with Mary, telling her that buying this house was a bad decision and ending with, "And Steve agrees with me!"

"This is a great location," I went on. "You can walk to downtown whenever you like." He did like downtown Los Gatos—with its quaint buildings, mostly occupied by boutique shops, pubs, and restaurants. He and Mary had strolled many times through the shops on a lazy weekend or had dinner or just met up with friends for a drink.

He nodded and turned to me with a pained expression. He felt ashamed, he told me, spending that much money on a house. His father, who had passed away earlier that year, had earned less money his entire life. Being the sole beneficiary, John had received the remaining lump sum of his father's work: $187,399. "My dad taught a class earlier that day, died of a heart attack in the evening as he walked home from campus." John accused himself of merely pecking at a keyboard and ordering a few people around.

We stood there, in the middle of the street staring at the house. "What's crazy is that I can buy this same house ten miles that way," John said, pointing east, "and pay a third of the price."

"Or less," I noted. "But you wouldn't be in Los Gatos."

"No—though roughly the same view and weather."

"So what you're really paying for here is the privilege of living around other people who are able to pay that much."

"Yep," he sighed. "A million dollars for the privilege of living among people of a certain socioeconomic status."

"I hope they're worth it."

He took a sweeping glance at the street, searching for neighbors who were at the moment invisible, and who would likely become familiar via perfunctory waves and courteous smiles and the occasional sidewalk chat. Finally, he shook his head in slight despair. "Who borrows a cup of sugar anymore?"

A car headed toward us and we stepped away from the middle of the street. After the car passed, I asked, "How's the inside look?"

John shrugged. "Beats me."

"You haven't seen it?" I said through a laugh, thinking he was pulling my leg. But he didn't answer. "Seriously?"

Though Mary had walked through it the day of the open house, John hadn't been inside at all. An old man still lived there. The real estate agent had arranged for John and Mary to view it on Saturday. Like he was staring down an opponent in a boxing match promo, his arms crossed, his face stern, his eyes fixed on the house, John said, "I'll wait to make my final decision until then."

Chapter Nine

December 18, 1999

STARING OUT THE WINDOW OF J. B. FLANNIGAN'S, about to tip my glass for the last bit of beer, I spotted a blond woman in a red dress with a long gait, who seemingly unveiled more leg with each stride. Standing outside the pub, four or five antsy men ogled her as she went by. She briefly turned their way, smiting them with a glare of contempt.

That's when I realized that the blonde was Lauren. And the man walking next to her was John. They had emerged from the Los Gatos neighborhood, directly from John's house, not more than a couple blocks away. It was quarter after six on the night of the housewarming party, and seeing John strolling into downtown with Lauren really startled me. What was he doing heading into town with Lauren?

Dropping cash on the table, I raced out after them. By the time I got outside, they had turned the corner. I pursued with a slow, dignified jog and found them as they entered a crowd in front of a dessert shop, Lauren plowing through, while John veered into the street and around the mass of people.

Following John's path, I had just cleared the crowd when they split up. John continued down the sidewalk while Lauren turned and crossed the main street. I wasn't sure what to do: follow Lauren and "accidentally" run into her or catch up to John. I went after John, but before I could get close enough to call out to him, he disappeared.

At that hour, most businesses unrelated to food and drink—the furniture store, the knickknack shop, the clothing boutique—were closed for the day. Penny University, a coffee shop, was open, and that's where John was, standing in a short line.

The coffee shop was not even half-full, and the only ones who should have been in there at six o'clock were lonely poets making impotent verses out of their self-agony and people who planned to eat dinner closer to midnight. Two tables not that far apart had sad couples with books and coffee cups between them. One man near the back engaged in a hushed conversation with himself.

"Hey!" I said. John hadn't seen me approach.

He turned, and having flinched slightly, he forced a smile. "What the heck are you doing here?"

"I should be asking you that."

"I'm just getting coffee."

"Aren't you supposed to be at a party right now, or did you find out you weren't invited after all?"

He barely laughed. "The coffee is for the party. It's a long story."

"Oh yeah?"

"The bartender forgot to bring coffee."

"Doesn't seem that long of a story. And who cares if there isn't coffee anyway?"

A bitter laugh came out. "There's a lot more to it."

"Like what?"

The customer at the counter finished. "Mary," he said simply, before walking up and ordering a pound of coffee.

"They have Greek coffee here," I said after seeing it on the handwritten chalkboard menu.

"Where do you see that?"

I pointed. "Right there. They call it Turkish coffee, but it's really Greek."

"Of course," he said. I did, as a habit, appropriate as much as I could in the world to Greece.

As the coffee was being ground, I said, "So what about Mary and the coffee?"

He told me about it: Mary had wanted to hire full-service caterers, but when he nixed the plan as unnecessarily elaborate, he was punitively given the task of finding a bartender. The problem, slight as it may have seemed, was that Mary insisted that the bartender serve coffee. The bartender had brought the coffee maker and dispenser but not any coffee. "Don't mention any of this to Mary."

"No, I won't," I said. "But is Lauren going to keep quiet?"

His eyebrows lifted. "You saw us?"

I nodded.

He sighed. "She saw me heading over here and decided to tag along." He had this agonized look that I recognized—he was considering confessing something. I didn't press him, only affirmed with a gentle grunt. "What's worse," he said after a few seconds, "she started this crazy talk, that it could have been her hosting the party tonight instead of Mary." His voice was breathy, nervous, but this was all a little boastful, too, the knowledge that he could have had Swede 11.

"Good thing Lauren doesn't know that you actually went into SGF that night to meet her."

He grimaced. "She does know."

"You told her?" I said.

"Not intentionally." He looked away briefly and then said, "Remember that night a few months ago, when the four of us went out to dinner to celebrate Mary's new job? And then afterward we came back to the apartment."

"Yeah, of course," I said. "Though I didn't go back to the apartment with you guys."

"Oh, that's right. Well, anyway, when we got to the apartment, we drank some more, and Mary fell asleep on the couch."

I nodded.

"I hadn't been smashed like that in a long time," he said, shaking his head. "I shouldn't have said anything to Lauren. Honestly, I don't exactly remember telling her, but I must have."

I wanted to ask him why he had done it, and then scold him for how stupid he had been. But I knew the reason. Alcohol was certainly part of it. But it was also Lauren. She had this way of extracting pity, usually something about her dad's dying when she was young. And even though she wasn't living in a ghetto, you sort of felt sorry for her, an exiled princess who lived disgracefully in a shingled-sided apartment complex with mature trees in Campbell.

The girl returned with John's grounds. When he had finished paying, we walked a few steps toward the door. "And she hasn't said anything to Mary, right?"

"No! Mary would be really hurt. She'd never forgive me. You know the rivalry those two have. I'd kill Lauren if she said anything."

It was true. I didn't know any other "best friends" who affectionately despised each other as Lauren and Mary did, simultaneously joyful and dispirited in each other's successes and failures. I had known siblings who acted this way, but siblings couldn't choose. Friendships lacked this familial handcuff, yet there it was.

"Hopefully it won't come to that," I said sarcastically.

"It'd be self-defense, anyway."

Initially I had taken the *I'd kill Lauren* as that everyday innocuous threat. But this second idea was unusual—it showed some thought. Especially strange for John, who was almost always good-natured. After a scoffing laugh, I said, "Self-defense? What are you talking about?"

"Because I'd kill myself if she told Mary."

"Come on. When did you get so dramatic?" I said, slapping him hard on the shoulder. "Where did Lauren go anyway?"

"To Vic's for a drink. I'm supposed to swing by and pick her up on my way back."

"I'll go get Lauren. You go home," I said, more sternly than I had intended, though not necessarily undeserved.

His eyes narrowed on me. "You still interested in her?"

I immediately spurted a sarcastic laugh. "Still? I never was." That was sort of a lie. If given the chance, I would have had to be tied to the mast to refuse her. I knew that. But I had never been given the chance, so it was easy to deny. "Except maybe that night from outside the window at SGF. But now I know her too well."

John gave out a grunting laugh. "It'd be great if you could keep her away from the party tonight."

"You want me to do that? I can."

"No, you can't. At least not for very long."

"You wanna bet?"

"Yeah." His tone was defiant.

"Let's make nine o'clock the over/under."

"Nine? Okay. Sure," John said. "Let's bet dinner. A nice dinner."

"Great." I pointed to the coffee bar. "But I'm getting myself a cup of Greek coffee before I go."

"Suit yourself," he said, and turning to leave, he added, "Enjoy your *Turkish* coffee."

"I'll call you tomorrow with all the details."

He guffawed derisively and then walked out.

My coffee, which I had ordered extra strong and sweet, came out really sweet and really hot. I sat down by the window and blew into the espresso cup. I thought about John and his harsh reaction to Lauren—the self-defense bit and all that. He wasn't serious, but he hadn't exactly been joking, either. Though I didn't think for a second he could actually do it. I wondered, then, if there was something else he wasn't telling me.

As I got to the bitter end and the thick bottom, two women eased in front of the window, smoking cigarettes. They were probably stragglers from the bar two doors down. A couple of twenty-year-olds entered the coffee shop, stood there looking for several seconds, and then left. The wispy edges of cigarette smoke seeped in.

Lauren was waiting—well, waiting for John, not me. I swirled what remained of the thick coffee around the cup and flipped it onto the saucer. It was a habit. If my Greek aunt had been there, after waiting a few minutes, she would have turned the cup over for a reading. I got up and left, leaving my future unknown.

Chapter Ten

GETTING TO VIC'S BREWERY proved harder than a four-minute walk from the coffee shop. I was nearing Vic's, thinking that I'd have to buy Lauren a few drinks when I realized that I didn't have my wallet. I rushed back to Penny University, hoping no one had snatched it. Fortunately, it was exactly where I had left it, off to the side of the register.

It wasn't like me to leave my wallet somewhere, but while I had been handing over a five-dollar bill to pay for my coffee, the cashier put a tray of small lemon squares in front of me and offered me a sample. I set my wallet down and took one. I mean, who passes up a lemon square? Especially since I hadn't had one in a long time, and my grandmother made the best ones. These rivaled hers, a near-perfect balance of tart and sweet, a thick bright yellow lemon curd on a not-too-thick butter-cookie crust.

That taste diverted me straight back to vacations at my grandparents' house in Florida. I only have fond memories of them, of my grandfather carrying me on his back, my grandmother's bountiful vegetable garden, working on puzzles on their dining room table, and my grandfather's simple magic tricks.

When the cashier handed me my change, I put it in their tip jar and promptly forgot about my wallet.

My cup was still there, too, at the table, upside down on the saucer. It would have been perfect for a reading now. Even though I worried about a restless Lauren leaving Vic's to return to the party, I picked up the cup and looked at the rim near the handle. The first image I saw was a dark, distorted figure. A person. I set it back down, leaving the tainted fortune behind.

Crossing the street, I saw a couple walking away from the front window of an art gallery. On my way to Vic's the first time, the same couple had been perusing the artwork. I slowed at the gallery to check out what the couple had been admiring. The painting in the forefront was a smeared cityscape warped by rectangular overstrokes. Behind that painting, were others, an impressionistic fruit bowl, a woman in a straw hat walking along the beach, and a painting of an old man staring off to nowhere. Farther back, lurking in the dim light, I saw a one-eyed monster struck by a spear in its eye. But when I took a second look, I saw what it really was: a painting of a martini with a single, oversized olive.

The gallery, like most stores, was closed for the day. Still, many people strolled and stopped to gaze at display cases and inside stores with their night lights on. As I passed these people and stores, my eyes were drawn to a woman—actually, it was her pale-fire hair that first caught my eye, and then her swaying walk, the clack of her heels echoing against the cement. And then I noticed the man with her, a short man with dark hair, balding.

I turned away.

They were still at enough of a distance that I couldn't say for certain that it was *them*. It was rather dark—only a soft glow from the festive trees lining the street reached the sidewalk. And as often as imagination plays tricks, filling in the contours left out by low light and separation, I concluded that it couldn't be them. It didn't make sense. For lots of reasons. First, this was Los Gatos, far from the offices in San Ramon. Second, and worse, he was fifty years old and she was barely half his age. Still, I didn't take a chance to find out. Instead I faced the shop I was near and got close to their unusual window display.

It was a bakery, and there in the display case, an enormous gingerbread man stared back. The biscuit was the size of a two-year-old, big enough that it might have fought back if bitten. And even if it couldn't defend itself, there's something amiss about eating a gingerbread man: either it's a symbolic form of cannibalism or else you're the devious fox at the end of the fable.

I heard my name called out. It was a familiar voice that instantly struck a nerve at the back of my neck. I turned slowly, preparing myself for what I already knew.

There he was, F. Jake Fitzgerald, wearing a suit and tie. With him was Joanna (yes, Swede 7), wearing a high-neck halter dress, a long black gown that narrowed around her body with a fair side slit up the leg.

"What are you doing here?" *What are you two doing together?* was what I really wanted to ask.

If I hadn't witnessed this—Jake and Joanna there together—I would have certainly chalked it up to another F. Jake tall tale.

"I'm here with Joanna. We're attending a wedding. Do you know Joanna?"

I nodded a bit indecisively. "Yeah, sure, I've seen you around. But I don't think we've actually ever met. I'm Steve."

She gave me a bright smile. "Sure. Of course I know you." *You're that creepy guy who gawks at me every time I walk down the hallway at work. And you rummage through libraries looking for me on book covers!*

Jake pointed behind me. "That's one huge gingerbread man!"

"I know! I was checking to see if it was real—I mean edible."

"Is it?" asked F. Jake.

"I don't know," I said. "I think so."

Joanna shook her head. "That cookie would bite back."

We all laughed. I had never been this close to Joanna. She had perfectly straight teeth and a great smile, and suddenly she seemed more accessible to me. A real person, not just a face and figure that I lusted after when I saw her strutting down the hallway.

"Where's this wedding?" I asked.

"Just around the corner up there," Joanna said, pointing. "The ceremony just ended. They're setting up the reception now, so we decided to go on a short walk."

"Terrible about the layoffs, huh?" Jake said.

"Yeah," I said, and not wanting to dwell on it, I quickly asked Joanna, "Whose wedding is it?"

"My friend from college," she said.

Jake raised his hand like a Boy Scout taking an oath. "I'm her plus-one," he said, adding a smuggish smile.

This is the only person you could think of to go with you? I would have gone with you!

"This is my fourth wedding this year," Joanna said.

"You're at that age," Jake said. "When you're my age, the only weddings you're going to are retreads in Vegas—divorced friends getting remarried."

That made me cringe inside, Jake's bringing up his age. But that's how he was, a light-hearted, gregarious personality.

Joanna laughed. "Oh, come on."

"I've only been to one this year," I said. "John's wedding."

"Oh yeah," Jake said. "It wasn't that long ago, right?"

"About two months ago. And he just bought a house. Not far from here. Just a couple blocks from here, actually," I said, pointing in the direction of his house. "That's why I'm here. He's having a housewarming party tonight."

"Good for him. Tell him I said hello," he said with a genuine grin. "And tell him congratulations on the wedding and the house."

"You should stop by later." I immediately regretted the invitation. I didn't want them there, and probably neither did John. It wasn't that John didn't like F. Jake. He did. But he very much separated his private life from his work life. As far as I knew, I was the only person who was part of both circles.

"Yeah, maybe we will," he said, looking at Joanna. "If there's time and it's okay with you."

"Sure, of course," Joanna said, her answer a little more polite than her tone indicated.

I gave them directions and we parted.

They were unlikely to show up, I figured. But if they did, hopefully it would shock and amuse John more than irritate him.

Chapter Eleven

VIC'S HAD TWO ENTRANCES, a side door that went directly into the restaurant's bar, and the front entrance, which was on the other side of the building near a parking lot. The door to the bar was blocked off by a large crowd, a mixed group of men and women interacting in a rambunctious way, their loud talking and laughter echoing down the side street. I remained on the opposite sidewalk and opted for the front entrance. The side street was quite dark, lacking the lights in the trees, and as I crossed the street, my foot landed awkwardly on the edge of a large pothole. I didn't twist my ankle, but it took me a few steps to shake it off.

Vic's was mostly a thirty-to-fortysomething-aged crowd. It was too expensive for the younger and too loud for the older. At least that was my assessment of it from the first and only time I had been there—the evening when John showed me the house and asked me to play the "guess which house is mine" game. The restaurant, also a microbrewery with several brewing awards posted on the wall, was a large room with lots of exposed wood and polished concrete floors. Tall cedar columns and pitched trusses formed a high ceiling. The acoustics were mostly awful, and if the dim lighting was meant to hush voices, it didn't work. The ruckus from the bar reverberated throughout the restaurant.

The glossy maître d', who had just taken a sip of something, set the glass down inside the podium and briefly pressed her thumb and index finger to the edges of her lips. I pointed behind her, and she returned a quick smile.

As I headed through the restaurant toward the bar, a woman sitting in a booth stretched out her hand. I started to go around her extended arm, thinking she was confusing me with waitstaff, but she yelled out, "Excuse me." I stopped and gave her an expectant look. She was in her late thirties, and the man with her, who was a bit older, appeared to be agitated.

"Sorry to bother you, sir," she said, "but you seem like someone who enjoys a good steak."

I glanced down at myself, in a ridiculous gesture, wondering what it was about me that made her think that. Looking back up at her, I said, "I do, but how do you know?" There was an explosion of *yays* from the bar.

She smiled and shrugged. "I need your help. Should I get the prime rib or the ribeye steak?"

"I've already told her that they're the same cut," the man said.

"But they have such different tastes and textures," she said.

"They're just prepared differently," he said.

"Go with the pork chop," I said. "It's excellent." That's what I'd had the time I was there with John.

"Great," the man said. "Another choice."

"I better go before you select your wine," I said and continued on. That's when I faintly heard my name being called out. I turned and saw Lauren sitting in a booth one aisle over.

Lauren stared at me with a slightly disapproving frown as I slid into the bench. "What are you doing here?" she said. There was a martini glass in front of her.

I let out a heavy sigh. "I ran into John at the coffee shop, and he asked me to come over and walk you back—he had to rush back to the house." I quickly added, "And I could really use a drink," since my goal was to keep her there.

Her face fell. "Pfffff." She shook her head in disgust. "I swear, he's so afraid of Mary, it's pathetic." She drained the rest of her martini.

"Were you planning to get something to eat?" I said, reaching to grab the menu lying open in front of her.

She shrugged. "All I've eaten today is a yogurt. I was waiting for John before ordering appetizers."

"Well, let's order some," I said, even though I was completely stuffed from my dinner at J. B. Flannigan's. "How about . . ." My finger scrolled down the menu. "Beer-battered onion rings and . . . fried artichoke hearts and . . . fried pickles."

"Gross. I hate pickles."

"Okay. What about crab cakes?"

An almost imperceptible smile appeared and disappeared. She shrugged. "Okay."

The waiter came to the table, and I ordered the appetizers and a glass of wine. I asked Lauren if she wanted another martini. "Sure," she said.

The waiter left. Hands folded in her lap, Lauren let her gaze drift to the bar, where people were clearly having a good time. She was disappointed to be stuck with me, and I nearly felt sorry for her. Though it was hard to believe she'd have succeeded—never mind the impropriety—at stealing time with John while he had an event going on at his own house.

"Some of your friends from SGF should be at the party tonight, right?" I said, trying to cheer her up.

"I guess so."

"You don't sound too excited."

She shrugged. "Who cares? I see them all the time."

"You don't like them?"

"Mary likes them. I put up with them." She expounded that they were "poor girls" who believed their proximity to SGF's clientele made them part of the upper social class too. For all her pretenses and affectations—her clothing, which she got discounted from SGF and her car, the 1959 Mercedes roadster that had belonged to her late father—Lauren didn't have money either. But she did have it for the first fifteen years of her life.

"They're all hoping to meet some rich guy. I mean, look at Mary."

Except this wasn't true of Mary. When Mary started dating John, his stock options were worthless. Besides, Mary didn't work at SGF anymore. She had left the clothing store a few months earlier and started working at SmartMile as market researcher.

I didn't correct Lauren. It would only have served to irritate her. Even now, knowing her absurd contempt for others, her face mesmerized me, and I couldn't help but study her as if it were my last chance to take her in. Her nose pointed out firmly, though not unusually so, and blended back with such perfect ease that it seemed it wasn't even there. Her cheekbones were high and slightly raised, and her eyes were large, round, and elusive in color—depending on the angle, or perhaps her mood, they were blue, green, or gray. Her skin, even there in the dull light, shone lustrously.

"Why are you staring at me?"

"Huh? Oh, sorry, just thinking."

"About what?"

I improvised. "On my way here, I ran into someone I knew. Two people, actually."

"The two you were talking to over there?" she said, pointing in the direction of the woman who had stopped me earlier.

I laughed. "No, I don't know them at all."

"Why were you talking to them?"

I explained, and then said, "The people I ran into were going to a wedding reception. Anyway, the girl is about your age, and her date—or rather the guy she brought with her, to be more precise—is at least fifty."

"I went to a wedding last weekend."

"With a fifty-year-old man?" I said—sarcastically, of course.

She pursed her lips. "No. It was my cousin Mona's wedding. She's five years younger than me, but she's pregnant."

"So does that make you next in the family? To get married, I mean. Not pregnant."

Her face soured. "The only one I ever wanted slipped away."

I didn't know exactly what she meant by that, but I froze, thinking that she was talking about John. The waiter returned just then carrying our drinks. Our appetizers would be brought out in a minute, he promised.

"Anything interesting happen at the wedding?" I asked. "You know, drunk uncles, etcetera."

She leaned forward, and the low scoop of her red dress fell open slightly. "The groom groped me."

"What!" It was hard to believe. The chump wearing the tuxedo stands out, and there are far too many witnesses to pull off a stunt like that.

"It was a slow dance and his hand kept touching my boobs."

My eyes instinctively drifted to her chest, as if verifying evidence of the assault. "On purpose?"

She leaned back and crossed her arms. "No, on accident. How many girls have you accidentally felt up?"

"So what did you do?"

"I kept pulling his hand away, of course," she said. "If there's one rule I have, it's never get involved with a married man."

Lauren should have been angry that any man, regardless of his marital status, had molested her. All of this struck me as totally incoherent: telling John that it could have been her instead of Mary hosting a housewarming party, and her plan to strand John at Vic's for an extended period of time. And then this supposed rigid standard against adultery. I didn't understand her.

The appetizers arrived, and Lauren jumped at the crab cakes. I stuck my fork into the plate of onion rings and corralled a few onto my plate.

"Speaking of weddings, I can't believe John didn't make Mary sign a prenup," she said before taking a bite. "Mmm. These are delicious."

"How do you think she would have reacted if John had served her up a prenup?"

"If she really cared for him, she would have signed it. I would have. No problem."

It was as if Lauren had given this quite a bit of thought. Then it struck me: It wasn't so much that she was interested in John. Her aim was to disrupt Mary.

Finishing my glass of wine—the wine layered over caffeine from the Greek coffee and the two beers I'd had earlier—a jittery and irrepressible mischievousness fell over me. Without consequential thought, I tugged on the thread to see what would unravel. "So you know about the night he met Mary at SGF, huh?"

"You mean that he went in there to meet me and not Mary. Can you believe that?"

"Yeah, I was there."

"You were?"

I laughed. "I'm the one who dared him to go talk to you."

"What?" She smirked and shook her head. "He didn't tell me that part. It's just like Mary, though."

"What is?"

"To take something that wasn't meant for her."

I looked at her with a doubtful glare.

"I lived with her for three years, okay? So I know. My stuff went missing all the time. Eye shadow. Lipstick. And she always ate my leftovers."

"Well, your leftovers are safe now," I said.

"Don't be a jerk. I don't mean just food and makeup. I can't think of anything right now, but it happened all the time. Believe me."

I grabbed the plate of artichoke hearts and slid a couple onto my plate. "Okay, I believe you," I said without any conviction.

She glowered at me. "No, you don't. Everyone thinks Mary's a saint."

I didn't respond to her and instead ate one of the artichokes. "These are really good," I said. "Especially with this sauce. You gotta try one."

"I got one," she said.

I glanced down at her plate, but there were only crab cakes.

"The perfect example of Mary stealing what's not hers."

"Okay. What?"

"It was that night, the night the four of us went out, whenever that was, back in August or September."

"Yeah, August," I said.

"Right. Anyway, remember the story about the married guy sucking up enough nerve to come talk to me?"

I nodded.

"Mary told you guys the story. But it was my story to tell!"

I didn't remember who had told it. "Yeah, I guess that's not cool."

"Not to mention that Mary kept interrupting us when we were talking. Remember?"

I nodded, reflexively, but it was John who had interrupted us more often than Mary.

"Why did you go home so soon that night?" Lauren asked. "I thought you were having a good time. Were you upset about something?"

The four of us had never gone out again, even though I had asked John. Since it had started getting close to his wedding, I didn't press him. "It was a crazy night. I think I was tired from work that week, that's all. But I guess you all kept going, huh?"

"Yeah—well, John and I did. We stopped at one more place after you left, and then we went back to the apartment. Almost immediately Mary dropped on the couch." She pulled the plate of artichokes and grabbed a couple. "I can barely remember what happened after that."

"What do you mean by that?" I asked, my voice faltering.

"In my defense, he wasn't married yet."

"What!"

She smirked. "Don't ask about things you don't really want to know."

Was this what John was really afraid of? Did something happen between them that night? That *I'd kill Lauren* comment suddenly struck me as more than an idle threat. It was hard to believe. Impossible to believe.

"Relax. Just kidding," she said in a flat, cool way.

We stayed quiet. I know what I wanted to believe, but I didn't know what to actually believe.

I suffered a detachment of sorts. A numbness. After a few minutes, I said, "You ready to go to the party?"

Lauren sighed. "Sure, after I finish these."

When the bill arrived, Lauren gathered her purse and left for the restroom. After paying, I headed there, too.

Chapter Twelve

THE RESTROOMS AT VIC'S were near the bar around a corner, away from the noise of the rambunctious crowd. In the restroom I encountered a glassy-eyed, stocky man who was around thirty years old. I asked him if he was part of the lively group at the bar. "Guilty as charged!" he said, and then explained that it was a bachelor party that had merged with an unrelated bachelorette party.

Walking back into the restaurant, there was no sign of Lauren, so I leaned against the wall near the women's restroom. Standing there, my eyes settled on a piece of "artwork" on the wall. An unframed canvas tortured with splatters of symmetrical black paint, a project that might have easily been completed by a five-year-old—splayed paint on one side, folded in half and then opened back up. If it had a meaning it eluded me. If it was a Rorschach test, it was Pamplona's most agitated running toward me.

The restroom door swung open. I straightened, ready to leave. But it wasn't Lauren. It was a few seconds later that I heard Lauren. Faintly. I rested against the wall, across from the charging bull, remembering what Mary had told me about Lauren. A secret that she didn't want to reveal . . . Lauren came out a couple minutes later.

"How long have you been waiting there?" she asked, her mouth shrunken and her eyes narrowing.

I shrugged. "Not long," I said.

She stammered a sort of confession. Her hand fell to her stomach. "I don't think I can handle cream sauce anymore. You know, that sauce for the artichokes."

There was a cream sauce on the crab cakes, too, but I didn't remind her of it.

Making our way to the side entrance, we entered the sea of people at the bar. Lauren moved swiftly through the throng. I maneuvered and bumped my way around the crush of bodies and stuffy air and alcohol and rambling talk. After escaping into the cool night air and catching up to Lauren, I told her what I had found out in the restroom.

"I don't ever want to hear about another bachelorette party in my life," she said.

"I thought you had fun at Mary's."

"Fun? Mary had fun," she said. "I was stressing out. I was working hard to get things right, and from the get-go, almost nothing did."

Of course I didn't confess that John and I had so much to do with her distress that evening—the town car that arrived ten minutes before the limousine, causing much confusion; the obscene cake replaced with Hello Kitty; the missing champagne in the limousine, replaced with sparkling apple cider;

the mouse in the wastebasket after they all arrived home drunk. And then the cruelest of all: the drink Lauren got at the Caravan. It must have really shaken her up when the bartender handed her the Ice Pick, a vodka drink, "compliments of Kurt." Lauren had nearly sought a restraining order against Kurt, an ex-boyfriend.

Though I wanted to brag about all of it—well, not the drink from Kurt—I said nothing. Almost nothing. I couldn't resist poking her a bit, so I asked how they had kept figuring out where John and I were going that night. We ran into them twice, at the first bar, and the second-to-last bar. "It's hard to believe it was just a coincidence. Did you have someone following us?"

Lauren scoffed and asked how we had pulled off our "stunt."

At the first bar, when no one was looking, Mary had winked at me through the crowd. She asked me later how we'd done it. "Lauren told us everything," I said, and then I explained how John had snooped around the apartment and found a notepad where Lauren had written the name of the limousine company and the bakery. And how I had gotten a coworker to call Lauren up, pretending to be from the limousine company, asking to get a list of bars they planned to go to that night. Lauren had complied, listing out every bar in order. Everything else fell into place from there.

We were quiet as we crossed the main boulevard and headed down the street that led to the neighborhood. This was where it had all started a couple of hours earlier, when I spotted Lauren and John across from J. B. Flannigan's. My car was parked in an adjacent parking lot, and I told Lauren that I had to get it. I didn't ask if she wanted to go with me. She just said, "I'll see you at the house."

As I crossed the street, walking toward the pub, a group of men were standing outside eyeing Lauren. This was a different bunch from earlier that night. I was thinking that I probably shouldn't be driving, but it was a very short drive, so I figured it would be all right. As I passed by the group, through a haze of cigarette smoke—a few of them were smoking—one guy said, "Hey, man. Hold up."

I kept walking. I wasn't sure it was meant for me, and if it was, I didn't know any of them anyway. And my shoes weren't untied.

"Hey! Did Lauren put you up to this?"

It startled me, hearing Lauren's name. Not only that, but the man's voice had a strong accusatory edge to it. I stopped and turned around. "Do I know you?" I said in a testy tone.

This man, wearing a battered black leather jacket, roughly shaven, with short hair, balding, was probably younger than he looked. So I guessed early to mid-thirties. The other men with him were about that age, maybe a little younger, and suddenly all of their eyes fixed on me. This felt hostile, and the scales went against me. If J. B. Flannigan's had been a real Irish bar, I would have immediately started down the alleyway. But this was Los Gatos, and the worst that could happen was a few stretched collars.

"Kurt," the man said. He stepped toward me. I had to disguise my flinch when he stuck out his hand.

Assuming this was *the* Kurt, the ex-boyfriend that Lauren had told me about, after hearing all the stories of stalking and psychological abuse and attempted violence, I wasn't sure whether I should take it. But I didn't really know him except from her stories, so I shook his hand, if only to de-escalate the situation.

"Steve," I said.

"Did she put you up to this?"

"What do you mean? Up to what?"

"She knows this is one of my hangouts."

"Just a coincidence, I think," I said. "Are you her ex-boyfriend?"

He nodded. "Are you walking to your car?"

"Yeah."

He made a minor gesture at his friends and said, "Mind if I go with you? I want to tell you something."

Once we had turned the corner and were in the alleyway that led to the parking lot, Kurt said, "Where is she going?"

I hesitated. Then I said, "To her car."

He shook his head. "Lauren does whatever Lauren wants. And gets away with it most of the time." I suppose he meant the sign that said neighborhood parking was for residents only. "She's trouble, man. How long have you been going out with her?"

Not sure what to make of this—jealous ex who didn't want to see anyone else with her or some sort of revenge act—I told him that he had it all wrong and that I was only a friend.

"Look, you've got to be careful with her. She's crazy."

I stopped walking. "That's rich, isn't it?" I said.

"What do you mean by that?"

"She was going to get a restraining order against you."

"What!" His laugh was loud and obviously sarcastic. "It was the other way around, man. She kept showing up at my jobs. That's what I thought she was doing here now."

Who to believe here? The stranger I'd just met or Lauren, whom I didn't trust? But the facts didn't go Kurt's way. For all her faults, Lauren was gorgeous, and it was barely credible that she had been stalking this man, a scruffy thirtysomething with a visible gap in his front teeth. I wanted to ask him if he had money, but he'd said *jobs,* so I immediately took him for some type of construction worker or tradesman.

"She even threatened me if I didn't get back together with her." His voice faltered. I pitied this man for a second. And then I thought of it as kind of ridiculous. Lauren? Sure, she could argue with privileged demand. But physically threaten?

He composed himself. "Anyway, she did it just to hurt me."

Did what? But I didn't feel comfortable asking. I said nothing.

"Just look in her purse before you get too far along with her. Maybe it'll change your mind."

Two things fought to come out at once: *What should I be looking for?* and *I'm not seeing her.* Instead I fumbled the words and some incoherent gasps came out.

He threw a hand in the air. "Anyway, no one can accuse me of not telling you." Turning, he shoved his hands into his jacket pockets and drifted back toward his friends.

I thought about stopping him. Find out who was telling the truth. But I knew it would have been useless. Was he actually going to admit to raising a nine iron to her? Or calling her up in the middle of the night and threatening to kill himself? Or trolling her at a bar, ordering her a drink called the Ice Pick? No, that had been me and John. And suddenly I wondered if the joke wasn't on us, that Kurt wasn't the fiend that had been described to us after all.

In the car, I gripped the steering wheel tightly. My head spun dizzily. It was more than just the alcohol. It was the encounter with Kurt and that mystery about Lauren's purse. What could possibly be in her purse that would scare somebody off?

John's house was close; a couple of turns and I'd be there. But the night scene enclosed on me like tunnel vision, and a block stretched for a mile. I started feeling trapped in my car, as if there weren't enough oxygen, so I stopped before reaching Mistral Avenue and rolled down the windows, swallowing deep breaths of cold air.

As I approached the house, cars lined both sides of the street. I stopped next to Lauren's car. The top to her Mercedes roadster was down, and a large, rectangular box sat on its end on the passenger seat. Lauren stood on the sidewalk and said, "Where have you been? Go park and help me with this."

The right side of the road was full of cars, up until near the end of the street, so I decided to turn around. Mistral Avenue ended at a street that ran perpendicular, and I made a wide U-turn in front of a large line of junipers—the shrubs shielded the house facing the intersection from oncoming car lights. I squeezed between a Saab and the driveway of a small, white two-story house.

The din of the party echoed throughout the neighborhood. I crossed to Lauren's side of the street, and as I got close to her, an old cat cut in front of me between two cars, blissfully pointing its tail upward. The cat, a gray tabby, thin, brought back memories of my cat, who went missing right before I left for college. I bent down to pet the cat, imagining wildly that this was her, two thousand miles away and twenty years old. Its purr rattled deeply as I scratched its head and petted its back. Lauren stood staring at me with hands on her hips.

It was just past seven thirty. I considered my bet with John, the bet I was about to lose. A bet he wanted to lose and that I was now throwing. If I told Lauren about my encounter with Kurt, that would delay things for a while. *What's in your purse?* A furious Lauren would undoubtedly stomp back to J. B. Flannigan's to confront him.

Lauren huffed, "Do you pet every animal you come across?"

I turned around but the cat was gone.

"That was Argos," I said.

"You know that cat?"

I laughed. "No. It reminded me of my cat from long ago."

"I don't trust guys who like cats," she said.

I shook my head at her and pointed at the large box sitting in the car. "What is it?"

"It's a housewarming present."

"I thought the invitation said, 'No Gifts.' There was even an exclamation point after it."

"What invitation? Maybe I wasn't invited." She laughed. "It's more of a joke than a gift." She smirked.

"It's quite a large joke." The box, wrapped in thick brown paper, was about two and a half feet tall and a foot wide. It weighed about thirty pounds. I set it down on the sidewalk.

"What's in here? A little boy?"

Lauren laughed. "No, but that'd be even better—it's a vacuum cleaner."

"You bought them a vacuum cleaner?"

"You don't get it? Didn't John tell you the story about the vacuum cleaner?"

I shook my head. And Lauren explained. After moving into the house, John found a vacuum cleaner in the entryway closet. For what he had paid for the house, he had expected a housecleaner, but instead he only got a vacuum cleaner. "But the vacuum didn't even work," she said, finishing the story.

"That's funny, but seems like an expensive joke."

She shook her head. "It's half hers. This is the old one from our apartment. Mary keeps the boxes to everything."

I helped her put the top up on her car. "You drove all the way over here with the top down?"

"I had no choice. It wouldn't fit with the top on, and the trunk is too small. The heater in this car gets super hot, so it wasn't too bad with the windows up."

She secured the top and locked the door. She walked over to the trunk, opened it, and closed it again.

I had lifted the box and was walking over to Lauren when she slid her hand to her chest, tucking the key beneath her dress.

"That's an interesting place to hide a key," I said.

"I'm not hiding it." She lightly patted her right side. "It's right here."

"Where's your purse?"

"In the trunk—that's another thing Mary stole from me. My red clutch purse. A perfect match to my dress."

"She stole it?"

"Yeah. We used to share it. She took it with her when she moved out. I only have a silver clutch that doesn't match my shoes."

I glanced down at her shoes. The black shoes . . .

"So I had to go with a black handbag, which doesn't go with this dress."

I didn't really understand. "It's hard to be a woman."

"Shut up."

Chapter Thirteen

THE HOUSE AT 316 MISTRAL AVENUE stood out from the other houses in the neighborhood. Besides the white Christmas lights strung along the eaves and tiny lights around trees and over bushes, every indoor light was switched on and every window visible. Other houses along this stretch had closed shades or dim yellow lights illuminating their porch. A few had Christmas trees in dark living rooms, but none of the neighbors had strung lights on the outside of the house, except one, which had wrapped a strand around their main window. Seen from an airplane, 316 Mistral would have looked like a firefly in full glory.

With the lusty laughter and loud talk that spilled into the street, I got the feeling we were entering the grounds of a traveling carnival. I swear my nose even caught a whiff of sugary air, that pink smell of spun cotton candy. I inched my nose to the box and sniffed.

"What are you doing?" Lauren asked me.

"Oh, nothing."

I followed her up the steps to the front door, wondering how I was going to lift her car key. There was only one way, which was no way. (I confess the idea tantalized me.) But what could possibly be in Lauren's purse? The more I thought about it, the more I thought Kurt was just playing me. I didn't care to be duped, but even so, I couldn't help wondering if there really was something to see. Only one idea came to mind: she carried a weapon. A knife? A gun?

Lauren opened the door, and as we walked inside, I expected an onslaught of loud chattering and stuffy air. But it was more like an unappreciated museum. The noise from outside barely carried in. "Let's put it in here," Lauren said, opening a door to the left. It was John's office. This was the first time I had actually been inside his house. He had intended to invite me over, but he said between unpacking, fixing some things around the house, and getting ready for the party, there hadn't been any time.

John's office was pristine. It looked and smelled like a room in a model home. There was an executive desk with a leather office chair and a bookcase. A thin rug covered most of the dark hardwood floor. I set the box down next to the desk. Lauren held a book in her hand, a paperback. "John reads these?"

She gave a scoffing laugh and then showed me the cover. I grabbed the book and stared at it. It was the surprise John had promised. And what a surprise it was! On the cover, with her head turned back slightly, her cleavage barely contained in a red velvet dress, held from behind by a shirtless bad boy, was Joanna. Her blond hair was pulled formally into a bun, a coiled wisp of it dangling youthfully down her face. That slightly curled upper lip of hers suggested an apprehension at this impropriety, her white-gloved hands covering his hands—to pull his hands away or clutch them tighter? A lady stung by wanton desires, unprepared for the onslaught of this man in low-slung ragged pants. "John and I know her!" I said, pointing at Joanna. But when I looked up, no one was there.

I set the book back on the desk, leaving it for John to surprise me later. Closing the door behind me, I crossed the entryway and went into the living room. The Christmas tree caught my eye. I greeted three women sitting on a couch with a friendly smile and firm nod and an inaudible, "Hi." The ceiling, ten feet high, sucked up any passive voices. The tree was tall and magnificent, adorned with white lights and all glass ornaments. Except the tree topper. Touching the ceiling, a perfectly placid angel wearing a purple robe observed all from up above, the large room with a fireplace and the two couches with a glass coffee table between them.

I overheard one of the women saying how exciting it was that the other was having a baby. She said how wonderful children are. The third woman agreed and said her two boys were the best kids anyone could ask for. "They're so much fun!"

The living room was an enclosed room, so after admiring the Christmas tree, I headed back to the entryway. A hallway went through on the right, and stairs to the second floor on the left. I walked down the hallway, past the dining room. The table in there was full of finger snacks, and three or four people were in there grabbing food. No fruit tarts from what I could see, but I didn't go into the room to look more closely.

The hallway passed another small hallway to the left that led to a bathroom and a bedroom. I went through an opening and entered a large space, a kitchen and then a family room and a small eating table. The kitchen had a massive square island. To the left, there were steps down. And at the far end, a door led outside. Still no Mary or John. I took the steps down into the lower level.

The lower level felt cramped compared to upstairs. John had told me about this—the finished space had not been included in the official square footage because the height between the floor and the ceiling beams was a hair under seven and a half feet.

It was here that I found John, talking to a priest and another man who looked vaguely familiar, perhaps someone who had attended the wedding. Neither John nor Mary was Catholic, so the priest threw me.

Once John noticed me, his eyes darted from me to his watch. He shook his head ever so slightly as he kept to his conversation. I went over, and he introduced me to the priest, Father Thomas, who seemed young for a priest, probably mid-thirties. He wore a heavily cabled, gray cardigan over his black shirt and collar. The other man was introduced as Gerald. He wore a sport coat too large for him and baggy jeans. Gerald's wife worked with Mary at SmartMile, John explained.

John told them that we used to work together and then said, "Steve is Greek Orthodox." John caught my sidelong glance and added, "We were talking about religion."

"Really? I thought religion, politics, and talking about Y2K were taboo at parties," I said. It was true that I was Greek Orthodox, an inherited trait rather than a studied, chosen faith, though that made it no less true.

"Definitely Y2K," John said with a wry smile.

Father Thomas, whose connection to this party was still unknown to me, said, "A friendly discussion. That's all."

"I was just explaining," John said, "that agnostics and atheists don't really exist."

"Atheists don't exist?" I repeated. "That's ironic."

"They're just procrastheists like me." Evidently John had already explained procrastheism to them.

Procrastheism. A term John had coined to describe his spiritual life. It wasn't that he didn't believe in God. He did. Firmly. And he especially believed in God's omnipresence. And the only way he knew how to deal with that—that is, live without the fetters of conviction while God watched—was to postpone thinking about God altogether. Just as with any other chore or task, he was simply procrastinating, setting it in the back of his mind, willing to deal with it later.

"There are no atheists in the foxholes of Bataan *or* in the Shady Lane Nursing Home," John said definitively.

"John is the unofficial head of the procastheism movement," I said. "Followers would elect him to be their leader, but they haven't gotten around to it."

Father Thomas chuckled, and Gerald bared his small teeth.

"You laugh," John said. "But it's either I'm living this life, or I become a monk and live in a monastery. There's no in between for me."

Gerald said, "I think some people don't believe in God." He turned toward Father Thomas. "No offense."

"None taken."

"The better question is, does God believe in you?" John said.

Gerald, briefly holding a quizzical expression, said to Father Thomas, "Even the pope affirmed evolution a few years ago, didn't he?"

A patient smile appeared on Father Thomas's face. "Sort of. It's roundly misunderstood."

"What do you mean?"

That smile remained on the priest's lips, and I could tell he was holding back a long sigh. "Well, he basically acknowledged evidence that transformations occur within species, but not that one species evolves to another."

"Yes, but—" Gerald started.

John interrupted. "If a bunch of monkeys were dropped off on an empty planet, you believe that you'd find humans walking around after a million years," he said to Gerald. "The truth of it is, if you dropped off a bunch of humans on an empty planet, you'd eventually come back to find monkeys running around."

Father Thomas smirked, and Gerald chuckled.

"Hard to argue with that," I said.

Gerald nodded.

"I see you got the pool table," I said, pointing.

John looked over as if confirming it was still there. "Yeah, just got it last week. That's literally the only furnishing I personally selected. Everything else is Mary's doing." John rattled the ice in his glass. "You guys should play. I'm going to get another drink. Can I get any of you anything?"

Gerald lifted his half-empty glass and said he was fine. Father Thomas shook his head.

"How about some coffee?" I said.

"Shut up," John said, shaking his head.

"There's coffee?" Father Thomas asked.

"As a matter of fact, there is. Yes."

"I could go for a coffee," Father Thomas said.

"Irish?" John asked.

Father Thomas smiled. "Black will be fine. Thanks."

"You?" John said to me.

I told him that I'd go get something for myself a bit later, and he left.

Father Thomas pointed at the pool table and asked us if we wanted to play.

"I haven't played billiards in years," Gerald said.

"Yeah, me neither," the priest said.

"Maybe ten years," Gerald said.

"Yeah, it's been a few years for me," I said, which was vaguely true. I didn't confess that John and I had played regularly at a nearby bowling alley when we worked together.

"Should we play cutthroat?" I said, so the three of us could play. Father Thomas nodded, but Gerald's expression let on that he didn't know the game. I explained the rules.

As I set the cue ball to break, Gerald said, "Look at me. Drinking rum and Coke and playing a game called cutthroat."

I shook my head. "Why not?"

Gerald explained that he was a high school principal, and I understood he was being facetious about the cutthroat reference, but I still didn't understand the part about drinking. I asked him about it, and he explained that he didn't drink in public: "You know, if someone recognizes me and sees me drinking hard alcohol. Appearances and all that."

It struck me that this was why Gerald was down there in the quiet basement, drinking where no one of consequence would see him.

I leaned down and broke the set. Nothing fell into a pocket, and Father Thomas, who was up next, eyed his options.

Gerald said, "I have this Catholic friend . . ."

Father Thomas looked up from the table and nodded.

"Actually, someone I went to school with," he continued. "He and his wife are single-issue voters. They always vote for the candidate who is against abortion."

There was the slightest wince from Father Thomas. "It's an important issue for many Catholics."

"Yes, I understand that. But why vote on a single issue?"

"I think it's more complicated than that," I said. "Aren't you forced to be a single-issue voter if you're really passionate about something? We live in a representative democracy after all, not a direct democracy."

Gerald gave a single nod. "You're right, but in the case of abortion, the Supreme Court decided that long ago. So why would you choose a representative based on an issue they have very little influence over anyway?"

I almost brought up Henry Renfro's Supreme Court supermajority idea as a response, but I remembered that it was actually irrelevant for this discussion.

"Then why do candidates bother to take a position on it?" Father Thomas said.

Gerald smiled. "Fair point."

Father Thomas eyed his shot and finessed the twelve ball into the side pocket. He called his range.

"I would just think that poorer Catholics," Gerald went on, "would be more interested in economic equality, not in allowing the rich to get richer."

"Isn't discussing politics on that list?" I asked Gerald.

"What list is that?"

"Things you're not supposed to do in public? Like drinking."

Gerald grinned. "Yes, you're right. But since it's just you two, and neither of you have kids at my school . . ." He took a quick sip from his glass.

Father Thomas struck the cue ball hard, nailing the eight ball wildly, which collided with several other balls.

"You're up," I said to Gerald.

He set his glass down on a long, narrow table against the wall. He asked which ball he should hit. I explained the game again, and he considered it for a minute.

Father Thomas brought up college football—probably to stop Gerald from bringing up politics again. We discussed the controversy that occurred each year with determining the best football team. As we played a second game (Father Thomas won the first one, and I was pretty sure it hadn't been as long as he had let on), he went on to say that he thought money was ruining college sports. Too much attention, meaning more money for programs and more money for coaches.

I didn't confess how much I actually did bet on college sports. Without making eye contact, I nodded ambiguously and muttered in agreement with him.

John returned, holding a short glass of whiskey in one hand. In his other hand he had a bottle of rum and a white mug, gripping the handle with two fingers.

He set the bottle of rum down on the table. "This is for you," he said to Gerald. John handed the priest his coffee. "And you, if you want to add a splash to your coffee."

Gerald nodded. "I won't ever have to leave the basement."

"What did I miss?"

I told John that we were playing cutthroat.

"You missed our discussion about politics," Gerald said.

"Good. I don't care much about politics," John said. "Too much of a team sport."

Gerald either didn't listen or didn't care. "We were talking about single-issue voters—"

"I can sum up all politics in one graph," John interrupted. He bent down and started using his finger as a writing implement. The plush gray-brown carpet was like velvet, changing shades depending on which way it leaned.

He drew an L shape, then wrote a dollar sign at the end of the L and wrote *God* at the top of the L. Then he drew a curve that started high near where he had written *God* and went downward toward the dollar sign. "The vertical line represents how religious a person is. The horizontal line is how much money they have. To the right of the curve is, well, the Right, and to the left is the Left . . . That's it," he said, straightening up.

Gerald walked around and regarded it for a few seconds—we all did.

"So if a person cares more about their religion than how little money they have, they will more likely vote for a Republican?" I asked.

John nodded. "Exactly."

Gerald nodded. "Interesting. But if that same person is less religious, let's say, then the likelihood that they vote Democrat goes up."

"Yes."

"Where does a procrastheist land on the God scale?" I asked.

"Depends on their age," John said. "The older they get, the higher up on that line."

Gerald rubbed his chin. "I'm sorry to say," he said to the priest, as if parenthetically, "people are going to church less and less. That's the trend." He pointed to the right of John's handiwork. "I've got to think that the Right will shrink over time."

Father Thomas set his cue stick on the area that was left of the curve. "Except these people over here are aborting their children."

"Whoa!" John exclaimed, barely holding down the sip of whiskey he had just taken. "Thomas!" he got out in a raspy voice, and then coughed. He cleared his throat. "This is why you don't discuss politics at a party."

"Though a little blunt," I said, "you're kind of on to something. I mean you'd have to assume there's some kind of hereditary predisposition to political beliefs. You know, kids mostly picking up their parents' politics."

John cleared his throat again. "I'd say that's mostly true—not a hundred percent. Maybe seventy percent. Something like that."

"Which means conservatives shouldn't be trying so hard to stop abortion," I said. "Insert that into your next homily, Father. See how that's received."

With a minimal, abiding smile, Father Thomas gently shook his head. "That would be a bit Machiavellian, wouldn't it?"

Gerald sighed. "I need more rum."

John used his foot to erase his drawing. "Mary just vacuumed down here. I don't want to get into any trouble."

I held out my cue stick to John. "Take my place. One through five," I said.

"Where are you going?"

"Get myself a drink. I'll be back," I said, though I had little intention of coming back.

Climbing the stairs, I stopped near the top, having spotted Mary in the kitchen sliding a tray into the oven. There were still about a half dozen other people congregating around the kitchen island. Mary was wearing a sexy yet fun cocktail dress in a dark purple color. Spaghetti straps curved around her neck, leaving her shoulders bare. The dress had a band around her waist, and the rest flowed down to an inch below her knees. Her high-heeled sandals had crossed straps and were a glittering silver. When she spotted me, a dagger struck my gut, as if she had realized that I'd been staring. But she smiled widely, and all of that went away. She called my name and approached me as I finished the few remaining steps. "Where have you been?" She hugged me.

I didn't know if she meant that night or more generally. The last time I had seen her, she was getting into a car with John the night of her wedding, to the roar of the revelers bidding them farewell. And even though I had been the best man, she had hardly spoken to me at the wedding or the rehearsal dinner. I knew the wedding was demanding and overwhelming, but I couldn't shake the nagging thought that she had been avoiding me.

"I've been around," I answered vaguely. "The house looks great."

"Thank you! I'm so glad to see you."

"Looks like you have a good turnout."

"A lot of people from my work showed up. More than I expected, which is nice. I haven't really been there for that long, you know."

"Free alcohol helps."

She laughed. "Yes, it does."

"So how do you like your job?"

"Love it. I think this is the start of my career in marketing."

"So you like your new job. That's good," I said, unable to think of anything else to say. The setting threw me. Nothing came to mind, though I felt as if there were so many things that I wanted to talk to her about. It lacked any possibility of an intimate conversation. I wanted to whisk her away to mini golf.

"Yeah, so different from SGF."

"I can imagine."

"But I miss the girls."

"Are they here?" Besides Lauren, there were five others who worked at SGF. Not that I knew them very well, but I had spent a bit of time at their table and danced with all of them at the wedding.

"They must be outside." She placed her hand on my shoulder. "Can you do me a favor?"

"Sure."

"See that man over there? He's my boss's husband."

There were three people in that vicinity: on the gray sofa, a man perusing a coffee table book, and a couple, a man and a woman, who were together talking quietly to each other standing near the glass door that went outside.

"The African-American guy?" I said about the man sitting on the sofa, an empty wine glass in front of him.

"There's no African-American over there?" she said, smirking.

"That Black guy over there? That's not who you're talking about?"

"Yes, him. He's not African-American."

"He's not?"

"No, he's British."

I rolled my eyes. "So he's African-British."

She shrugged. "Is that even a term?"

"I don't know. Probably not."

"Well, would you go talk to him for me, please? I was going to ask John, but I haven't seen him in a while."

I didn't tell her that she must have just missed him going downstairs. "Sure."

She put her hand on my back. "Thank you so much. We'll catch up later, okay? I really want to. I've missed you."

"Yes, definitely," I said. I wanted to tell her I had missed her, too, but it was too true for me to sound insincere—not that I thought her insincere, but I was fairly certain she didn't mean it the same way I wanted to take it.

The *African-British* man, named Richard, was obviously British once he spoke. I told him my connection to the hosts, and he told me his. He and his wife were originally from Leeds. He came for a job, at a start-up that aggregated job listings. I knew about it; I had just seen their purple-and-lime-green logo.

"How does it make money?" I asked.

"We don't," he said. "Right now we're only concentrating on getting as many visitors as possible."

"And then what?"

He shrugged. "Not sure yet. There's lots of ideas. Charge for rankings, for example." He leaned toward me as if to let me in on a secret. "The goal is to sell the company well before we have to figure it out."

I nodded. "Interesting," I said, though I still didn't understand how a business could be started on that kind of premise. But it was, after all, a quickly changing world, and I still felt stuck in the old one.

We were both looking at Mary as she turned the corner with a plate of small appetizers in her hand. "My wife told me that Mary invited everyone working at their office."

"Yeah, I heard about that."

"How do you plan an event like this without making people RSVP? How do you know how many people are going to show up?"

"I have no idea. But do you really think having people RSVP helps?"

"Sure. Why not?" he asked.

"I don't know. If it's a wedding and you're asking people whether they want the chicken or fish, people respond. But a party like this? Only some people will say they're coming or not. Most won't respond at all, or they'll respond with an ambiguous, 'We'll try to stop by.' So you still don't know how many are going to show up. And besides that, some people who said that they weren't coming actually show up anyway."

"First off, if someone showed up who had said that they weren't coming, I'd kick them out."

I chuckled, very briefly. He held a steady frown. "You would? Seriously?"

"Absolutely."

"How about someone who didn't respond at all?"

He grimaced. "That's tougher. That would depend."

"On what?" I asked.

"Whether I liked them or not."

"But you invited them to your party."

Richard shrugged. "Mary invited everyone here. Do you think she really likes them all?"

Lauren immediately popped into my head. "Yeah, probably not."

"I don't think she even knows all of them," he said.

I nodded and then pointed to the coffee table book he had been flipping through. "What's the book about?"

"Subways around the world. Kind of interesting."

"I've always wanted to make a coffee table book," I said.

"Oh yeah? On what?"

"Gas station restrooms."

Richard laughed, "That would be different."

"Have you ever done a road trip in the US?"

Richard shook his head. "No, not had the pleasure yet."

"Well, I don't know what the UK is like, but a clean bathroom is like a gift when you're traveling."

He nodded. "It's no different. So you'd just take photographs of those restrooms and put them in a book? Is that the idea?"

"Yeah, the awful places. I'd go across the country and take pictures of each one. Write a little nostalgic blurb about how each contributed to a uniquely horrible experience."

Richard laughed. "That would be entertaining. Definitely. But I don't think there would be a big market for it."

"It'd make a good white elephant gift."

"White elephant?"

I sort of paused here, stunned for a second, unsure whether I should be embarrassed. I didn't know the origin of the term—*white* elephant. As if that had anything to do with anything. It was a knee-jerk reaction.

"Yeah, it's a gift exchange for Christmas where a bunch of people get together and swap gifts. Gag gifts are part of it."

"I know what you're talking about. Yes, a coffee table book about restrooms would be perfect for that."

"These books are more decoration than anything, anyway. You're probably the first person to crack open this book. I mean, I wouldn't call my book *America's Crappiest Crappers*. It would have a pleasant name, like *Famous Facilities Across America*."

"And the British version could be something like *Lost Loos of Britain*."

"Yeah, exactly. And people would buy them as long as they had nice covers. I mean, look over there," I said, pointing to five coffee table books stacked in a pyramid-like shape in the TV cabinet. "Only the size determined whether it made the cut. Content is irrelevant."

He nodded. "Yeah, you're right. Although . . ." He turned his head looking around and then stepped over to the cabinet. He rearranged the order.

Hungary

Jacques Cousteau

Escapes

After Eats

Man's Best Friend

"That's good," I said, chuckling. Then I took the book he was reading, *Underground*, and positioned it beneath *Escapes*.

Chuckling, Richard said, "Lovely."

Okay, so British men say *lovely*.

As I was centering the stack, a woman came in from outside.

"Hello, dear," Richard said.

"What are you boys up to?" she said, her eyebrows stern and her tone accusatory. We denied all involvement in anything. Richard introduced me to his wife, Jill. We spoke for a few minutes before I excused myself to get a drink.

The door to the outside might as well have been a portal, whisking guests between alternative parties. The inside was tame and slow moving, the noise from outside like a television left on in another room. Outside, it was louder, colder, dimmer, and by the eruptions of laughter, a lot more fun.

The yard smelled of manicured lawn. A large white tent covered most of it. Under the tent, round tables and chairs were set up, and with the tent's sidewalls, there were enough heating lamps and bodies—and alcohol, to be sure—to keep the area warm, nearly toasty. The whole thing was set up for a wedding, sans a chicken-and-Caesar-salad dinner.

After peeking into the tent, where partygoers were sitting at tables, standing around tables, and, in one case, standing on a table—the man, trying to touch the top of the tent, was being coaxed down—I headed to the bartender, who had been left outside between one side of the tent and the back of the garage. He did have a heat lamp near him, and I suppose he wasn't cold since he was actually moving around working.

There were a couple of people ahead of me getting wine poured for them. That's when someone bumped into me from behind.

I turned around and it was an older woman with outstretched arms. "Are you okay? I'm so sorry," she said, her breath warm and sweet. She placed her hands on my shoulders; it was unclear whether it was a friendly gesture or whether she needed help to hold herself up. Her silver hair grazed her shoulders. I would have initially guessed sixty-something, but on closer inspection her pale skin was still perfectly smooth.

"Fine. I'm fine," I said.

She wore a black top with long sheer sleeves. "I tripped on something there on the grass." We both looked down but there was nothing there to see except grass and her flat, patent leather black shoes.

"It's okay," I said, thinking she was tipsy.

"You're John, aren't you? I've seen Mary's wedding photograph on her desk." She spoke rapidly. "I'm Barbara, the crazy one with the doll collection. She must have mentioned me."

I didn't look anything like John, and as a joke, I almost went along. "No, I'm not John. John is a good friend of mine, though."

"I thought you looked familiar."

"Were you at their wedding?"

She shook her head. Then she told me about her doll collection. Five hundred and forty-two dolls.

"Wow. Children must love to visit your house."

She frowned. "No, no, no. No children. They destroy everything and don't respect anyone's property."

"But—"

"Last week, for example, I was at a shop picking out a doll to add to my collection. It happened to be the last one they had. I have two others exactly the same—it's sure to become a collectible. Out of nowhere this awful girl with pigtails runs out screaming for my doll. And then she began to cry."

"Like that's going to change your mind," I said sarcastically.

"Not a chance. And lucky thing for that doll, too. You should have seen the one this girl already had. It was so filthy, and she held it by her hair. Why give a precious object to someone like that?"

"What a brat," I said. I meant Barbara, not the little girl, but I intended it to be misunderstood.

"Yes, definitely. No appreciation of anything, that generation."

"Where do you keep your collection?"

Barbara explained that her "man friend" was allergic to cats, so she kept her townhouse for her four cats and left her doll collection there, too. It was stupefying to learn: a house just for cats and dolls when many salaried people at that time couldn't even find a place to live.

"Looks like you have it all worked out," I said. A group of three had crashed the bar, so I pointed to the house. "I better get back inside," I said with vague urgency.

"Oh, yes, of course."

My friend Richard was gone, but I was glad to see that Jacques Cousteau was still hiding underground.

"Steve!"

I turned around to find John smiling at me. He rubbed his hands together. "I have something to show you."

"What is it?"

"You'll see."

I followed John toward the wide hall.

"This is some party you have going on," I said. "There's even a wedding reception outside."

He laughed. "I know. It's totally overboard."

The doorbell rang. Worried that it was F. Jake, I quickly said, "You're not going to believe who I ran into tonight."

As he asked, "Who?" the front door opened, and a man, swarthy and balding, with a bit of a gut, came inside and closed the door. He held himself with a certain distinction—was it his clothes, a black turtleneck under a sport coat and slacks, and cap-toe Oxfords? Or was it some mannerism, his comfort with walking into a strange house?

"Jay! Great to see you," John said with a falsely overdone giddiness. "Come inside," he said, even though the man was already in the entryway. He handed John a bottle of wine.

Even though I didn't know Jay, I knew who he was. I'd seen his photograph on the company's website, the company where John worked. And John had told me plenty of stories about the man.

Jay Garvin was CEO and a dot-com billionaire, at least on paper. He hadn't created anything. He wasn't a founder of the company. He hadn't guided a fledgling company into becoming a profitable concern. Garvin had simply won the lottery, had been at the right place at the right time, taking the company through their IPO during the dot-com craze. Sure, he was a good showman, an actor. And with his self-assurance and unearned authority, he projected a fictional narrative to speculative investors, who were complicit in this uncoordinated Ponzi scheme.

Jay held out his arms out like Christ over Rio de Janeiro. "So this is what I helped you buy."

John faked an agreeable laugh and thanked him for the bottle. They shook hands, and John introduced me. His eyes brushing over me, Garvin took my hand as if he were a neurosurgeon, and I immediately loosened my overeager grip to match his slack one.

"I can see you have your hands full with guests. I was on my way to a charity event at Montalvo, and I thought I should stop by."

"I appreciate it," John said. "Come have a drink."

Garvin shook his head. "No, I really shouldn't. I need to be going." He looked at his watch. "I'm already an hour late."

John abruptly stuck out his hand. "Well, thanks for stopping by."

There was a long pause as if Garvin hadn't expected this—as if he had expected John to insist that he stay for a drink or perhaps tour the house or at least meet his wife. The man must have gotten used to subordinates pleading for his attention. Garvin, holding a surprised, mopey stare, cleared his throat and took John's hand. "Good seeing you, John."

"You too." John stepped toward the door.

My farewell and firm nod went unnoticed

"I'll see you next week," Garvin said to John.

"Thanks again for the wine."

"Of course," Garvin said and left.

John shook his head after closing the door.

"Quite the character," I said.

"It was Mary's idea to invite him. And I only agreed because I figured he wouldn't show up." He let out a long sigh before amending it with a chuckle. He handed me the bottle of wine. "Here, keep it."

I looked at the label. "Is this an expensive wine?" The bottle was from Carballo Winery, Napa Valley.

He didn't answer me. He held out his arms like Garvin had and mimicked, "So this is what I bought you." He shook his head in disgust and laughed again, then looked at the bottle of wine. "He owns part of the vineyard. It's probably good, but I can't drink it. It's been psychologically tainted." He gestured toward his office and said, "Let's go in here. I've got something for you."

"You're not going to believe who I saw tonight," I said.

He immediately noticed the package. "What's this?" he said, more to himself than to me.

I closed the door. "That's from Lauren. She had me bring it inside." I set the wine bottle on the desk. "Guess who I saw?"

His gaze remained on the box. "What is it?"

"I'm not sure," I said, which was truer than I realized. "I ran into F. Jake tonight."

"Huh? Where?"

"Downtown. Just a couple hours ago. And guess who was with him? You'll never guess."

"Who?"

"Swede 7."

"Joanna? No way!"

"F. Jake was her date."

"Get out of here! You're kidding, right?"

I shook my head. "Nope. In fact, I told them to stop by if they have time—I hope you don't mind. I'm not sure they'll make it."

"No, not at all. I just can't believe Swede 7 and F. Jake—maybe all those crazy stories of his are true."

I laughed. "Maybe we were wrong about him this whole time."

He smacked his desk with his palm. "Which makes this even better." He walked over to the other side of the desk and picked up the book, which was sitting upside down. He showed the cover to me.

"What! I can't believe it," I said, trying my best to sound genuinely surprised. I grabbed the book. "Where did you find it?"

"I did a little research on the internet . . ."

"I had totally given up!" I had quit hunting for her books at the library. (The last time I was there, swiftly picking over the latest releases, I was approached by a heavyset woman who whispered, "You shouldn't judge a book by its cover.")

I held out the book for him to take back.

"No, that's for you."

"Well, keep it in here in case she shows up. I wouldn't want to have to explain."

"Yeah, you're right," he said, taking the book. "She might think we're creeps."

I laughed. "So who's the priest slash pool shark?"

"Oh, that's Tom Coleman. He's an old college friend."

"Really?"

John nodded. "I hadn't seen him in ten years. He's at a conference out here, and he called a couple days ago. Wanted to know if we could get together tonight, so I told him to come out to the party."

"Maybe say a little blessing for your house?" I said.

"Two actually. The garage is detached."

I laughed. "True."

"Anyway, I did something for him a long time ago, and . . ." He looked away.

"What did you do?"

He shrugged and shook his head as if it had been nothing or he didn't want to say. But he did want to tell me or else he wouldn't have said anything at all. "I don't really like to talk about it."

I nodded gently and waited patiently for him to tell me, and he did.

John and Tom met in college. Once the thrill of newfound independence waned, their friendship thrived. Both wanted to "make it big," and they spent hours coming up with and discussing business ideas. But the two had very different motivations. Tom's father owned a large construction firm, and Tom wanted to prove to his father that he could make it on his own. John, whose father was a professor, lived more modestly, and John believed money equated to happiness.

During their junior year, Tom's girlfriend died in a tragic accident. He reevaluated his life, and he decided to go to seminary after college and become a priest. John asked him about their dream of making money. Tom suddenly saw things differently. "The only difference between the rich and poor is their art," he told John. John, half-angry, half-insulted, barely listened as Tom explained that even the poor in this country have shelter, food, a television, and a family portrait to hang on their wall. The difference, he claimed, could be accounted for in the quality and quantity of those things. "The rich hang original artwork."

"You've never been poor one day in your life!" John yelled back at him. But that wasn't untrue of him either. And though he hadn't grown up wealthy, it was never about what he didn't have; it was about what others had.

Still, this complete change of heart had struck John, especially since they had never even discussed religion.

Tom's parents, though Catholic, were extremely unhappy with the decision, and they stopped paying for school, forcing him to take out a loan in order to pay for his senior year. So when Tom went to join the seminary, he was refused until he had resolved his debts—the college loan and some credit card debt. Tom's parents must have known about the debt condition, John figured, and had cut him off on purpose.

John didn't have any money, either, so he couldn't have helped his friend even if he'd wanted to. He, too, had a bit of credit card debt to pay off. But once he got a job in California, he got more credit cards and took out cash advances. He cleared Tom's debt, and that was how Tom was able to join the seminary.

"Wow," I said after hearing the story. "And you're not even Catholic."

"Don't ever mention this to him," he said. His voice had cracked, which eased the admonishing tone. "He thinks the money came from an inheritance, from an uncle of mine."

"No, I won't say anything."

"So what happened?" John said. "I thought you were going to keep Lauren at the brewery until nine. You weren't even close." He placed Joanna's book in the small bookcase among his other books. The feathered font of *Sin of Omission* stood out between *The UNIX Toolbox* and a spiral-bound book, probably a user guide of some sort.

I lifted up my hands. "It's Lauren. She's antsy. Keeping her there for over an hour was a miracle."

"Where is she anyway?"

I shrugged. "Haven't seen her."

He pointed a finger at me. "You owe me dinner, man."

Walking over to the package, he said, "Let's see what this is." He unwrapped it carefully, removing the tape one piece at a time. He folded the paper back and a consternated expression appeared on his face.

"What is it?" I said.

"A stroller."

"Huh?" I eased over, and sure enough, it was a stroller, not a vacuum cleaner. "And car seat combo." I laughed. "That's a very strange housewarming present—wait, is Mary pregnant?"

"No! Of course not. I need to hide this."

"What's this all about?" I asked.

"Lauren's being provocative. She probably thinks it's funny."

"What's the joke? I don't get it."

John shook his head. "It's a dig at Mary—about being a housewife, the end of her career and all that." He slid the box underneath his desk as much as he could. He started for the door.

We walked out of the office and down the hallway. As we passed the dining room, I said, "Have you had a fruit tart yet?"

"No, not yet."

Luda came our way. "Mary is looking for you, John," she said in her serrated Russian accent. "Hi, Steve," she said.

"Hey, Luda." Luda was a friend of Mary's from SGF. She had stringy brown hair and strong cheekbones and hooded eyes—attractive as an exotic look. She wore a short, tight dress that most couldn't wear without appearing promiscuous. She eluded all that with hard stares.

"What does she want?"

Luda shrugged. "I don't know." She pointed to her right. "I really need to wee."

We heard a knock. "Would you mind getting that while I check on Mary?"

I nodded. "Maybe you ran out of coffee again," I said.

"Ha ha," he said and we went in opposite directions.

When I opened the door, no one was there. I stepped out to the smell of lingering cigarette smoke. It was dark, and my eyes adjusted from the bright lights indoors.

"Steve!" came from a man's familiar but unplaced voice.

At that far end of the porch, beyond the glow from the light in the living room, three people emerged. Lauren and another man were leaning against the railing and smoking. The other man stood opposite them. And that's when I realized that it was F. Jake.

I approached them. "Sorry. I didn't know you were here," I said to F. Jake, who was still wearing a jacket but had lost the tie.

"I just got here a few minutes ago. I haven't even been inside yet."

I introduced myself to the other man, Walt, a neighbor from a few doors down. How Lauren got entangled with these two—or how they got entangled with her—I didn't know.

"Is Joanna here?"

F. Jake shook his head. "No, she'll be by later. She was catching up with some friends, and I was just standing around, so I walked over."

Lauren asked me if I wanted a cigarette. I hadn't smoked in twenty years, though I nearly did, just to astound her. "No, I quit a long time ago."

"Good for you," Walt said, and then took another puff.

Lauren flicked ashes over the railing. She was more into the act rather than actually smoking. "He's a doctor," Lauren said.

"Medical doctor?" I said, looking at Walt.

He nodded. "Cardiologist."

"What about the smoking?" I said, too astounded to help myself.

F. Jake punched me lightly on the shoulder. "I've got a lot of friends in the medical profession," F. Jake said. "And I'd say that about a quarter of them smoke."

"If you include nurses, yeah, that's probably about right," Dr. Walt said. "It's horrible, I know. But these help me cope with the stress from my job."

"Seriously?" I said.

He nodded. "Stress will kill you faster than any cigarette."

"Ever think about changing jobs?" I said.

"What's he supposed to do? Go work in construction?" Lauren said.

Dr. Walt laughed. "True. I don't have any other skills. Though I wish I knew construction."

None of us have any other skills, I wanted to say, but I didn't.

"But don't worry," Dr. Walt said, looking at me. "I'll quit before it's too late."

"And how do you know when that is?" I asked, trying not to sound too incredulous.

"I'm forty-two and an average smoker. If I quit before fifty, I'll be fine."

Lauren pointed her cigarette at F. Jake. "You were saying a ranger showed up."

F. Jake rubbed his hands together. "Yeah, right. So out of nowhere this ranger appears, all angry, saying that he'd been tracking us for three days."

He was regaling them with a classic F. Jake adventure. How he had gotten to telling them this story, I didn't know. It was about a camping trip three or four years earlier in Arizona or

New Mexico. My mind drifted for a minute as I stared at Lauren's chest, trying to figure out how to get that key.

"Is that a serious offense?" Dr. Walt said. My eyes went to him, and that's when I noticed the wood-bead bracelet on his wrist. I knew why F. Jake had brought up this story.

F. Jake had his audience on the edge of their seats. He was a good storyteller. He had that smirk on his face, and after a long pause, he said, "No, not too serious. The ranger was Native American himself and was impressed that we had eluded him for so long. Not that we were really trying. The problem wasn't that we had veered onto a reservation. The real problem was that we were camped out on sacred land."

"Oh no," Lauren gasped.

F. Jake nodded. "We got a lecture for a good fifteen minutes. He even said the Navajo could kill us for trespassing, but I didn't believe it."

I didn't believe any of it, except that he went camping somewhere and got lost.

"Well, you didn't do it on purpose," Dr. Walt said, as if he'd known F. Jake for years.

"No, we didn't. We mistook a landmark and ended up in the wrong place. Good thing the ranger showed up, too. We might have been wandering for days. Anyway, after we explained everything, he sat down and had coffee with us." F. Jake stuck out his arm and pulled up his jacket and shirtsleeve. "And he was wearing this." There was a wood-bead bracelet wrapped tightly around his wrist.

"You killed the ranger and took his bracelet!" Lauren said.

Overeager laughter from both Dr. Walt and F. Jake.

"No, of course not," F. Jake said. "He took it off and gave it to me. Said it would protect us from danger." An Indian casino gift shop outside of Flagstaff was more likely.

"He just gave it to you?" Lauren asked.

"Yes! He said he made them. I tried to pay him, but he refused."

The cigarettes were getting exhausted, and so was I. "Will Joanna be showing up later?"

"I sure hope so. She's my ride back."

I pointed toward the house. "I'm heading inside."

"Yeah, I'll go in with you," F. Jake said. He turned to his new friends. "It was nice meeting you. I'll try to make it to your party next week."

"That'd be great. It's going to be a ton of fun," Dr. Walt said.

Once we were inside the house, I said, "What party were you talking about?"

"A New Year's Eve party—but it's also a demolition party."

"A demolition party?"

"Yeah, he's remodeling his house so he's letting people punch holes and spray-paint the walls. Sounds like fun, doesn't it?"

"You sure make friends fast."

He held his palms up. "I didn't do anything. Well, not really. I was just walking up the steps, when the blonde came out."

"Lauren."

"Right, Lauren. She asked me if I had a light. I said that I did." He pulled a gold lighter out of his pocket.

"You smoke?"

"No, it's my grandfather's. Honestly, I wasn't even sure if it would work. But it did. So I lit the cigarette for her and the doctor friend. Actually, it's ironic, because the last time I saw my grandpa, he was lying in a hospital bed, dying from emphysema. Right before he died, he shook his crooked finger at me and warned"—Jake's voice imitated an old man's hard whisper—"'Don't ever smoke, Jake. You are ultimately responsible for your actions.'" F. Jake cleared his throat. "Then the old man patted me on the head like he was firming the dirt after planting a seed."

"How old were you?"

"I was around ten at the time. And after he died I really believed he was constantly watching me. I'd ride my bike to the cemetery and visit his grave site and promise him that I would never smoke. I even went a step further and started a crusade to stop others from smoking."

"Really? What did you do?"

"I started stealing packs of cigarettes. From my friends' parents."

"Seriously?"

"Yeah, I even got caught once, and they thought I was stealing them to smoke."

"Oh no."

"Yeah, but it was only a phase and didn't last long. You know, childhood distractions and all that. Fast-forward a few years, my sophomore year in high school to be exact, and I was regularly smoking before and after school."

"Don't tell me you smoked the stash you'd stolen."

F. Jake smiled. "No, no. I had gotten rid of those."

"So you ended up being a smoker?"

"Only until my senior year. It was when I got this precalc teacher who was new to the school. He looked just like my grandfather. Spitting image. I was so guilt-ridden that I never smoked again. I found the lighter when my mother died, and I always carry it with me now."

"So why did you light their cigarettes?"

"That blonde, man. Come on. Who could resist that? I couldn't help it."

"Yeah, I get it . . . maybe this will help you feel better," I said, and took the pack of cigarettes out of my pocket.

He grabbed the pack. "The doctor's cigarettes! You stole them?"

I nodded. I had swiped the pack off the railing when no one was looking. "He won't quit before fifty. Who's he kidding? So I'm giving him a helping hand."

He put his finger to my chest. "You're the man!" He looked around. "Do you know where the bathroom is?"

I pointed down the hall. "Up there. First left. Can't miss it."

F. Jake's story of his precalculus teacher stirred a memory of my own, about my precalc teacher, Mr. Romans, a superb math teacher. Though I don't recall much about precalc, there's one lesson that sticks out. I could never fully grasp the concept of infinity and how one number on the number line was no closer to infinity than a lower number. Surely a trillion is closer to infinity than ten, I reasoned. One day I asked Mr. Romans about this. He grabbed an orange from his desk and made a dot. "Suppose that is one," he said, and proceeded to draw a line and then another dot at the end. "And suppose that's one million. Which one is closer to the center of the orange, Steve?" I protested, "But the center of the orange is not on top with all the numbers." He smiled and said, "Exactly. Infinity is not a number." He handed me the orange and patted me on the back as I left. I ate the orange and understood.

Chapter Fourteen

IT WAS A QUARTER TO NINE. Guests were like leaves scattered in the wind, though some got stuck in a corner while others re-assembled elsewhere. In the backyard, on my way to get a drink, I heard my name called. It was Mary, and I was excited that she had sought me out. As she approached, I saw that she had a determined expression rather than an interest in chatting.

"Would you please help me?"

I told her that I would, and she had me follow her to the garage.

She walked briskly toward the detached garage at the back corner of the lot. "So Lauren was really chatting up your neighbor, the cardiologist," I said after she had opened the side door.

She spurted a caustic laugh. "Walt? That's ironic." She turned the light switch on.

"What do you mean by that?"

The garage was smaller than it appeared to be from the outside, probably because it was lined with cabinets on both sides, and in the center of the garage was a car hidden under a gray cover. I was going to ask about it, but Mary started talking.

"I'm going to tell you something, but don't ever repeat it," she said, her tone matching her admonishing frown. "Not even to John."

I felt that closeness again, that intimate feeling I'd had a few months earlier when we were alone together. "No, I won't."

Mary closed the door. Her eyes dropped a bit. "Lauren has a heart condition."

"Seriously?" I said. "That's horrible."

"Yeah, spare me the grief."

I didn't really take Mary for being so unsympathetic. It shook me. And suddenly she wasn't exactly who I thought she was. "What?"

"It's her own fault."

"How can you say that, Mary?"

"How? She took fen-phen, Steve. Even after they started warning people about it, she continued to take it. And she was already thin. Can you believe that?"

Fen-phen. A couple years earlier, the popular diet pill had been exposed for its dangerous side effects and had been banned because it caused heart issues. "Really? How did she ever get a prescription?"

Mary folded her hands under her chin, tilted her head, and batted her eyes.

"She manipulated some stupid doctor?" I asked.

"Of course."

"Wow. That's crazy."

I was going to mention that Lauren had apparently moved on to bulimia (recalling Lauren's vomiting in the bathroom at Vic's), but I dropped it and instead pointed at the car.

"What's that?"

"It belonged to my grandfather. Take a look."

I pulled the cover partially off.

"MG, huh?" It was white.

"Sixty-six. He left it to me."

"The body looks to be in good shape."

"Pretty good, yeah. It's the engine that needs a little work. John's going to fix it."

"John who?"

Mary smiled. Those dimples appeared. "John knows about fixing cars."

"He does?"

"Yeah. I didn't know, either, until I had to decide whether or not I was going to take the car. John told me he worked on cars as a teenager."

"I've never heard that. But how did you get John to take it?"

"Why? What do you mean?"

"Isn't your grandfather dead?"

"Oh, *that.*" She pulled the cover back over the car. "He thinks that this is my grandmother's car, and that she's no longer driving it."

"You lied to him?"

"No," she said. "It's technically my grandmother's car."

I shook my head at her.

She approached the refrigerator. It was a six-foot-tall refrigerator with a top freezer.

"What are we doing?" I asked.

She opened the lower door of the fridge.

"I want to surprise John," she said. "You know it was his birthday on Thursday."

I knew his birthday was sometime in December, but I didn't know the actual day.

"Yeah," I said.

"I bought him a cake—well, two, actually, and that's why I need your help."

"I get it now. This whole party was just a cover to surprise John for his birthday."

Mary laughed. "No, but I'm sure he's going to think the same thing." She pulled out a quarter sheet cake and handed it to me. She reached in and took out another one. "Darn. I forgot the matches. Wait here. I'll be right back," she said, setting the cake on the workbench.

As I waited there, my eyes drifted to a blue tarp covering something rectangular about three feet tall. I set the cake down next to the other and pulled up the tarp. It was a generator.

Mary walked back into the garage with matches. "Okay," she said. "Let's hurry and light this. I've got Luda holding him up near the kitchen."

She lit the candles. I was holding the cake with the "5" candle, and Mary was carrying the cake with the "3" candle.

As we passed by the tent, Mary called out to people to follow her. People started calling other people and with hushed giddiness and shushes, they got behind us as if we were the pied piper.

"Let me put my cake down first," I said as we were about to go into the house.

Mary laughed. "Fifty-three? He's old enough as it is."

"Hey! I'm thirty-five."

We walked inside flanked by a crowd. "Surprise!" Mary yelled and everyone else did, too.

John turned around. His face was bright red. As we sang "Happy Birthday," more people came in from around the house, and more people packed inside. John stared at Mary with a false frown. He kissed her and then blew out the two candles. And I was completely jealous, just like on that first day I had met him. Who was this guy and what had he done to deserve all of this?

Chapter Fifteen

After the cake had been distributed—I never did get a piece—people started reassembling in their previous places. I had a conversation with a woman whom I didn't know—and whose name I never got or can't remember—about birthdays. She was short and had a peppy demeanor, probably a year or two shy of thirty. I explained that I had just turned thirty-five a couple of months earlier and that it had been the hardest birthday of my life.

"Why is that?" she asked me.

I explained that my father had died at seventy, and thirty-five was the halfway point. "So I just experienced the best part of life," I said. What lay ahead for me was the declining second half. At some point I would have children, which I described to her as the "embodiment of a death clock." After the children leave, ailments mount and the body falls apart.

My speech must have depressed her, or else she misunderstood my intentions, because she quickly left with some excuse about having to find her boyfriend.

I eased over to the kitchen island, where the cake had been. There was a smear of frosting left on the cake pad, and I ran my finger over it. I overheard one woman talking to another woman saying, "No, I'm done having kids. I couldn't risk having another boy. Boys are monsters." It was the woman who had been raving about her two boys earlier in the living room.

Stepping into the backyard again, I was determined to get that drink. I walked past a man who had a woman in a drunk embrace—his arm slung loosely around her neck—and the woman, who had become a crutch, was half-helping him into the tent. I wondered how many people would be plastered that night.

When I reached the bartender, who was as enthusiastic as ever, I ordered a gin and tonic—a glass of red wine didn't seem to be enough to keep up with this crowd.

With drink in hand, I peeked into the tent—no sign of Lauren—but at a table sat her coworkers from SGF: Luda, Claire, and Sherry. I stopped next to Luda. "Sit down." She grabbed my hand and pulled me to a chair next to her.

Claire, the manager at SGF, was in her late thirties. Her hair was short, brown-copper in color, spun in a tight perm. She had bronze skin and deep facial lines. From what I'd heard, she acted a bit like a mother hen to the girls, both admonishing and fiercely protective of them.

Sherry, a thirty-year-old, was pretty in a cute way—big cheeks, big eyes. She oozed this easiness about her. It was a mixture of her innocent mind and her constant smiles as she pretended to understand even though she was usually a step behind.

"You guys miss Mary?" I said.

They all nodded. "Yes, of course," Claire said.

"She was our buffer to Zmeya," Luda said. *Zmeya* was her nickname for Lauren. It meant "dragon" or "snake" or something like that.

I nodded. "Yeah, I get it."

We were talking about how fun John and Mary's wedding had been when dark-haired and slender Lynn, the final SGF girl, sat down across from me. She wore so much makeup as a habit that you couldn't resist questioning face paint as a practice.

Lynn looked around and then back at us. "Seen Lauren around lately?"

Everyone shook their heads. I didn't say anything about spending part of my evening with her.

"You're not going to believe where I saw her the other day," Lynn said.

"Where?"

"So my mom has been seeing a cardiologist for a while for a heart valve issue."

"Is she okay?" I asked.

"Yeah, she's fine for now. But at the building where she goes there's only cardiologists, except for one OB-GYN."

Lines instantly appeared on Claire's brow. "Okay, so her gynecologist is there. So what?"

"I saw her car there a couple months ago, too."

"She's pregnant?" Luda said.

Lynn made a shrugging-nodding motion.

"What?" Sherry said. "Why do you think that?"

"Who goes to their gynecologist more than once a year?" Lynn said.

"I definitely don't," I said.

That got a chuckle out of them, and then Claire said, "Hold on. Maybe she's got some sort of medical issue down there."

"Yeah, she's pregnant," Luda said, her sharp teeth emerging in delight.

What they couldn't come up with was the truth: that Lauren was really there to see a cardiologist. And I wasn't supposed to reveal that to them.

John came into the tent, and while they went back and forth—Luda swearing that Zmeya's breasts were bigger—he made eye contact with me. All the girls yelled and gestured to John to come over, and when he did, they showered him with happy-birthdays. Before it had all settled down, Luda urged Lynn to tell her story all over again.

Ignoring Claire's long sigh, Lynn retold her story. John, who was standing next to Claire, lost all color in his face. He sat down, the chair seemingly catching his fall. "How long ago was this?" he asked.

"The first time was two or three months ago. And then again this last week."

"But she's not showing," he said. It came out more like a protest than a doubt. "At least as far as I can tell," he added.

Lynn shook her head. "I didn't really show until after my fourth month. You wouldn't have known I was pregnant."

He stared off for a moment, thinking.

"How about the drinking?" I said. "She's been drinking tonight."

"Yeah," John said. "She's been drinking."

Luda waved a hand. "Pffff. Women in Russia drink godawful vodka for many, many months when pregnant."

There was a joke there about Russians, but I was afraid to make it.

John got up.

"Are you bored with us already?" Luda said.

"No, not at all," John said. "I just need to do something, and I'll be back. Actually, Steve, could you help me?"

I followed John outside the tent. When he turned to me there was a controlled panic on his face. That flippant remark from Lauren circulated in my head: *In my defense, he wasn't married yet . . .*

I downed the rest of my gin and tonic. As a friend, part of me wanted to assuage his fears and let him know that Lauren was not pregnant. But I also wanted to let him wallow in whatever torment he might have been going through. That he could ever do that to Mary made me sick.

"I need to get rid of that stroller."

The stroller. I had forgotten about that. It must have taken on a double meaning for John now. An insult at Mary and a veiled message to John.

"Why?"

"I told you before, Mary will be upset if she sees it. Especially now."

"Why especially now?"

He answered in a hard, angry whisper. "Because they're right about Lauren, she beat Mary at getting pregnant."

"I thought you said it was about—"

"Never mind that."

"You hid it pretty well under your desk," I said. "Don't worry about it."

He shook his head. "If Mary's giving someone a tour of the house and goes in there—why did you bring it inside anyway?"

I didn't particularly appreciate his accusatory tone. "Lauren told me it was a vacuum cleaner." I was going to add that even if I had known it was a stroller, it wouldn't have held any particular meaning for me, except that it was odd. But I left it at that.

"A vacuum cleaner?"

"Yeah, something about the previous owner leaving a vacuum cleaner in the closet that didn't work."

"Oh. Yeah, I did tell Lauren about that."

"Looks like you've been telling Lauren a lot."

His stance straightened, and his face tightened. "What's that supposed to mean?"

I shook my head. "Nothing. Relax."

The wrinkles on his forehead eased after a second. "She's been after me, you know."

I nodded, without knowing exactly what he thought he meant by it. The wind picked up slightly and the cool air felt good against my hot ears.

"Would you do me a favor and put that box in your car? Please," he said, in a pleading tone that nearly embarrassed me.

I nodded. "Yes." I shook my glass, the two small ice cubes that remained clinked pleasantly. "After I get a refill."

Chapter Sixteen

THEY SAY THE FIRST RULE OF A MAGICIAN is never to reveal the secret of a trick. In my book, the first rule of a true magician is to never reveal you're a magician at all. So this is breaking that rule, and it's also a sort of confession . . .

When I was younger, I took a serious interest in magic, eventually becoming a decent amateur magician, especially for my age. Then at some point during my mid-teenage years, my attention turned to pickpocketing. Not because I wanted to become a thief, but because it would elevate my skills as a magician. I became quite good at it, too. I could lift a wallet fairly easily—under the right circumstances, anyway.

It was about that same time that I stopped performing magic tricks. To anyone who knew me—my parents, my friends—I had given it up and retreated to an almost forgotten adolescent phase. But in fact, I hadn't given it up. All the time I was honing my skills. I'd regularly lift somebody's wallet or take a piece of jewelry. I'd always give it back, of course (or at least make sure they could find it). So if I wanted to be someone's hero for five minutes, I'd take an item off of them and find it later—"Gretchen, I found it! Your lost earring."

It was far into college before my days as Harry Collins completely vanished.

Waiting for John to come back, I pulled out *Sin of Omissions* from the bookcase, Joanna acting perfectly aghast. She was pretty, very pretty, but in a rotten sort of way—I knew nothing about her really. My remote view of her was biased by whatever preconceived notions are naturally attached to women who look like Joanna. What truly lay underneath that exterior, I couldn't really say.

Hearing steps closing in, I slipped the book back into the bookcase as John walked in. "All clear," he said. "But you have to go now. Mary is giving someone a tour upstairs."

I lifted the stroller box, still mostly wrapped, and we walked out of the office, surreptitiously, like we were up to no good. He opened the front door. "Do you need help?" he asked.

"No, I got it," I said and carried the box down the porch steps and to the sidewalk. My car was about five houses away.

As I set the box on the ground to open the car, I noticed someone walking on the sidewalk. Mistral Avenue didn't believe in bright streetlamps, and large trees blocked the little light that there was. It was difficult to make out the person's face, but the gait was unmistakable. It was Lauren heading back to the house. Where she had come from, I didn't know.

After dumping the stroller in the car, I chased after her. She crossed the street, but instead of going up the porch steps, she turned left and went toward the side gate.

I yelled after her, but she didn't stop.

The side yard was mostly dim, with a few landscape lights that ran along a narrow path of flagstone steps. The spillover light from the downstairs bedroom and from the high windows in the great room partly illuminated the area, too. The path was flanked on either side by bushes.

Before she reached the corner of the house, I cupped my hands around my mouth and called her name again. Loudly. She stopped and started to turn, and as she did, she stumbled. She fell sideways, and trying to regain her balance, she ended up in a bush.

It was quite comical, especially for Laruen, always pretentiously graceful. But I didn't dare laugh. I ran over to her. Her arms were elbow deep in rosemary. "You okay?" I said, bending over and placing my hand around her. I lifted her up.

She was in a daze and didn't say anything for a second. "Geez. You scared me, Steve!" Though she had been drinking quite a bit, her breath didn't smell of alcohol. It smelled of old mint. "You can't sneak up on someone like that."

"Sorry, but I've been calling after you."

"I didn't hear you." She brushed away needles that clung to her dress.

I folded my arms. My heart beat so furiously that I feared Lauren seeing the palpitations through my shirt. "At least you smell good."

"Shut up," she said, picking off the last few needles. "So what did you want to tell me? Or did you just want to get me alone to feel me up?"

I apologized and started an explanation about being clumsy, but then I let out a nervous laugh. Laruen's story about the handsy groom popped into my head. Maybe he had been trying to lift a key, too.

"What's so funny?"

"Nothing, sorry. I just wanted to ask you about that gift for Mary."

"Yeah, what about it?"

"Why did you tell me it was a vacuum cleaner if it was really a stroller?"

Lauren placed her hands on her hips. "You shouldn't have opened it. It wasn't for you."

"I didn't. John did."

"Oh. What did he say?"

"He said you were trying to upset Mary."

She rested her hand on my forearm. "It was a harmless prank. No big deal."

"Seems like more than a little joke."

Lauren withdrew her hand and crossed her arms. "Is Mary your girlfriend or something?"

"No, of course she's not," I said, sounding like a defensive fifth grader caught staring at a girl. "That's ridiculous."

"Then don't worry about it," she said, and turned and left.

I stood there for a few seconds, my heart still beating wildly. It had been a while since I had lifted anything. If I had been challenged that night to pickpocket someone's wallet, I would have given it a fifty-fifty chance. To snatch a key tucked in a woman's bra—impossible. But when I helped Lauren up, I had a split-second window. Stunned by the fall and trying to get up, and distracted by my hand lodged under her—high on her ribcage—as I pulled her off the rosemary bush, she didn't notice my other hand.

So as Lauren disappeared into the party's frivolities, her car key rested in my pocket.

Chapter Seventeen

MY FIRST THOUGHT was not to go to Lauren's car. I needed to get a grip on myself. I began to shiver—not from the cold but from the subsiding spike of adrenaline. I flipped Lauren's key around in my pocket and started for the front, passed the gate, and walked over the lawn to reach the sidewalk. I wandered to nowhere, trying to get my sea legs back. What had just happened with Lauren looped over and over in my head. *What if she had caught me?*

A few minutes later, having hit the end of Mistral Avenue, I stood at the corner and stared at a massive oak tree in front of the house on the opposite side of the street, wondering whether the trunk was large enough to stop the excessive chi running in that direction (I had recently watched a home improvement show and knew enough about feng shui to know that).

Longing for another drink, I made my way back. That's when I spotted Dr. Walt crossing the street toward the house. I gave a feeble wave before turning and heading up the walkway. I have no idea if he waved back, but it struck me that Lauren had come from that direction, too. I wondered what she could have been doing at Dr. Walt's house.

I heard Mary talking upstairs, and I considered going up. I still hadn't seen the second floor, but I needed that drink to numb my nerves. I made my way back outside and to the bar to get myself a gin and tonic.

As I tipped my glass to the bartender, about to take a sip, someone slapped me on the back, slightly knocking my teeth into the glass. I turned around and it was F. Jake.

"Hey, man," he said.

"Hey, Jake."

"Fun party, huh?"

I nodded pleasantly, and still reeling from that scene with Lauren, I took a swallow from my glass. "Yeah, great party," I said in a raspy voice.

"Slow down there, mister," F. Jake said, and asked the bartender for a cup of black coffee.

"Coffee?" I said.

"I was born in LA, man, not the Midwest." He rubbed his hands together. "I'm not used to this cold like you and John."

I lifted my glass. "This will warm you up faster than coffee."

He laughed. "Yeah, you're probably right."

"Actually, if it were fifty-five degrees during December back in Ohio, we'd be out in shorts."

"I'm sure."

"To tell you the truth," I said, "I don't know why, but California cold has a weird way of sneaking up on you."

"It's because people don't plan for it. People always expect the weather to be warm." F. Jake got his cup of coffee. He took a sip. "Mmm. This is good coffee."

I told him about John's misadventure with the coffee. "That's funny," he said. "You know, I haven't even seen him tonight."

"Didn't you see him when we sang 'Happy Birthday' to him?"

"No! I was in the basement. I figured it was for someone I didn't know. Besides, how often do you get to shoot pool against a priest?"

"Father Thomas."

"You know him?"

"Just met him today. Apparently an old friend of John's."

"Lost a hundred bucks to him."

"You did?"

He laughed. "No. But I would've if we had been wagering."

"I know. I don't normally think of priests as pool sharks."

"No," he said, shaking his head. "I'm sorry I missed John's birthday cake."

"Well, let's go see if we can find Mr. Gatsby," I said.

"Who?"

"You know, *The Great Gatsby*, when Nick goes to Gatsby's party but doesn't see Gatsby—until he mentions it to someone and it turns out to be Gatsby himself."

"Totally over my head, man."

I laughed heartily. "I thought you of all people would get that."

"Me? Why me?"

"Because you're related to F. Scott Fitzgerald." *It's the reason John and I call you F. Jake!*

"No, not me," he said. "My wife—my ex-wife. She's distantly related, like third cousins twice removed or something."

This revelation took me a long second to sort out. "So you took her last name?"

"What? No—oh, I see." He giggled. "No. It so happens that my last name's Fitzgerald. Come to think of it, she might have married me just to get my last name. She kept it after the divorce."

"Ah," I said. I really started to doubt my doubts about F. Jake. I had "reread" *The Great Gatsby* after I heard about Jake's connection. I hadn't read it since high school (if I had truly read it at all), and after finishing *Gatsby*, I decided that reading was a good thing. I began to read other books, selecting off a list purported to be the greatest novels of all time. John insisted *The Brothers Karamazov* was the greatest novel of all time—well, according to his father, the Russian lit professor—so I started reading a copy that had belonged to his father. It was a book full of *-ovs* and such terrible family dynamics that I really wasn't enjoying it that much.

So because of a poorly played game of telephone, Jake became F. Jake, and I began reading classics.

"Let's go find our host," I said.

As we started, a commotion erupted from the tent. Some laughter. Then Lauren shot out, her face burning hot with anger. A round dark spot stained the front of her dress as if she had been shot in the gut. And as Lauren walked away, we could see a smear—something white—on her backside.

"Too much to drink tonight, I guess," I said.

"She's awfully balanced to be drunk."

He was right. She walked briskly. There wasn't an insecure step. But that scene earlier in the side yard, she had been uncoordinated, even if I had startled her. "She's definitely had a bit to drink tonight," I said.

"Maybe she got that IV from the doc."

"What IV? What are you talking about?"

"You must have missed that part—that doctor earlier on the porch. He offered her an IV drip if she needed it. She complained of a headache from all the drinking tonight."

"What's the IV for?"

"Hydration. It's a hangover cure."

"That works?"

"Heck yeah. I used to hang out with this old army medic when I lived in SoCal. A bunch of us would go out drinking." He laughed, reminiscing. "We'd stumble home around three a.m., and he'd set us up with an IV . . . Wouldn't feel a thing in the morning."

"Really?"

"Yeah. And this doctor here said he had a special blend."

"Of what?"

"I don't know, he named a bunch of stuff, vitamins, anti-inflammatories, potassium—he said she'd feel even better than before she started drinking."

"He wouldn't do that," I said. "His reputation and all that."

Jake shrugged. "Why not? I mean, he's qualified. And I don't think he cares what others think." He winked at me.

He was right. And it would explain where Lauren had been when she was walking back to the house. She had gotten a spiked IV from Dr. Walt.

When we entered the house, I saw John with Lauren at the very end of the hall, turning toward the staircase. F. Jake was behind me and didn't see them as they disappeared. I wasn't sure if they had gone into the office or upstairs.

Mary came up the stairs from the basement with three women in tow. These were the same three who had been sitting on the couch in the living room earlier.

I introduced F. Jake as a coworker of ours at the phone company.

"Actually, John was my boss for a couple of years."

Mary introduced the three women, Mary's coworkers: Linda, Gina, and Paige. Gina was the one who had the best/worst boys. Paige was the twentysomething pregnant one. After Linda made a comment about how wonderful the house was, F. Jake said, "This kitchen is amazing. But I haven't seen the upstairs yet."

"Oh, let me show you," Mary said.

We all headed down the large hallway, the three women back to the sofa in the living room. Half of me wanted to rush past them and steal their spot.

I explained to Mary how I had run into F. Jake downtown. She said, "We almost had our reception at the Opera House, remember?" She turned and looked back at me.

I never knew that, but I nodded like I did. "Yeah."

The door to the office was open slightly and I peeked inside. No one was in there. At this point, I could have tried to delay Mary from going upstairs. I knew a freaked-out John was up there with a super-drugged-up Lauren. But I decided to let it unfold—as if I were watching a movie, I didn't try to warn the character on-screen who was about to be ambushed from behind.

The upstairs opened to a wide space, not just hallways and doors. "This is spectacular," F. Jake said. "Nice and open. So airy."

Straight ahead were double doors that presumably went to the master bedroom. But before the doors, on the left, was a sitting area with a wide opening. "This is the library," Mary said. The room was about fourteen by ten. It had a fluffy white couch on one end and a bookcase full of books on the other. A man I hadn't seen that night was standing in front of the bookcase, perusing the books. We exchanged pleasantries with the man. I don't think even Mary knew who he was. Again, a joke about Owl Eyes popped into my head, but it would have fallen flat with F. Jake.

"This is huge," F. Jake said as we entered the spacious master bedroom, a fireplace on one end of the room. Not even the king-size bed and two tall armoires could diminish the overall impression that the room was bare.

Suddenly John came out of the bathroom. When he saw us, his face instantly burned bright red. "Jake!"

"Hey, John. Long time." John came forward in an awkward, long step to shake hands.

John shuddered as he turned to Mary.

"This is Jake, honey. Have you met?"

"Yes," Mary said. She stared at him with a frown.

Then we heard it. Lauren's voice. It echoed from inside the bathroom. "John, these jeans are way too big. I need a belt."

"What's Lauren doing in there?" Mary asked, her hands on her hips.

"She spilled wine on her dress. I was letting her get something to change into," John said, the words clacking. "Is that okay?"

Lauren emerged holding a bunched shirt against her chest, her stomach and shoulders revealed, wearing jeans that were too short. "Sorry, I didn't know we had an audience," Lauren said. "Mary, where's that blue top you have, the pretty blue one that looks way better on me?"

I peeled my eyes away from Lauren to look at John, whose stare was fastened on Lauren's midsection.

Mary pushed past John, shaking her head. "You can't wear that. Let's find something else." Mary lowered her voice. "Something appropriate since . . ."

"I like this party," F. Jake said from the side of his mouth.

We stood there for some long seconds. "Mary was giving us a tour of the upstairs," I said to John, trying to move the heavy cloud that sat over us. At least I felt it.

John corralled us out of the bedroom. "So you're out with Joanna tonight, huh?" he said, masking his nerves with a forced jovial tone.

"No, not like that," F. Jake said. "She needed someone to go with her to a wedding. Kind of last-minute—her date bailed on her."

"Runner-up with Joanna is still winning in my book," I said.

"Come on, you guys," F. Jake said. "It's nothing like that."

John showed us one of the bedrooms; there was a queen-size bed with a thousand pillows on it and an en suite bathroom, bright and white. "The other three are pretty much identical," John said hurriedly. "Let's go downstairs and get something to drink."

Chapter Eighteen

When I opened the trunk to Lauren's car, I was only a little drunk.

It was ten o'clock, and one gin-and-tonic refill later. If I was going to do this, it had to be then. Soon enough Lauren would realize that her key was missing. That, and I didn't want people who were leaving the party to see me.

I held the trunk lid open with my left hand. It was cavernous, and completely dark. No automatic light came on. The only illumination came from the half moon and the streetlight, which was two cars away and partially blocked by a pine tree. I stuck my head inside the trunk.

"Leaving already?"

As I turned to see who it was, the trunk lid slipped off my hand and struck my head. Hard.

The next thing I remember, the blackness was receding while my name was being called repeatedly. Someone was holding me up.

"Oh my God! Steve, you all right? Steve?"

It was Joanna. Totally confused, I said, "You've changed your outfit."

"What? No. Are you okay?"

I must have conflated her with her book cover. "Yeah," I said, holding myself up. I hesitated for a second. "I'm all right." I touched the top of my head, where the metal edge had struck me. There was a swelling lump.

"Let me take a look."

I lowered my head and she felt around with her fingers. "I don't see any blood. You should probably put some ice on it."

"Yes, I will," I said.

"I'm so sorry," she said and then she bit her lower lip in an endearing, guilt-ridden way. "I didn't mean to frighten you."

"It's okay." I laughed. I was now regaining my senses, nerves starting to build. Not only because Joanna had interrupted me while I was snooping through Lauren's car, but also because it was Joanna who had interrupted.

"I like your car."

"Oh, um, it's not mine," I said nervously. "It's a friend's. Wanted something out of it. But yeah, cool car. So how was the reception?"

"Good. Bride and groom left pretty quickly. Jake's here, right?"

I nodded. "Yep. Jake Fitzgerald. No relation to F. Scott Fitzgerald, by the way," I said, punch-drunk—and maybe drunk-drunk.

She laughed. "Is this supposed to be one of Gatsby's parties?"

"Yes!" I said. "You would've gotten my jokes earlier."

"What jokes?"

"There was a guy inside, in the library looking at books—"

"Owl Eyes?"

I laughed as that image of Joanna on the cover flashed in my head. "Yes. I'm so surprised."

"At what?"

I recovered with a lie. "That no one else knows these references."

"Actually, I have a secret theory about that book. Kind of crazy. You want to hear it?"

"That's why I came over tonight," I said in a slightly mocking voice, as if repeating a line in a movie.

She laughed. "See, I get that. But my theory isn't about the butler's nose."

I smiled. "What's your theory about?"

"It's kind of crazy . . . My theory is that Nick was in love with Daisy Fay."

"Really? I've never thought of that before."

"I mean, think about how he describes her."

"That's interesting," I said. "But what's Nick's plan? I mean he never tells Daisy that he's in love with her."

"You know that part where he says that his honesty is his cardinal virtue?"

I nodded. "Yes."

"Well, it's definitely not honesty, we all know that. It's patience. He's just biding his time, trying to earn enough money in the bond business. He knows Tom is cheating on Daisy. It's not like he discourages Tom from cheating. He lets it happen. Witnesses it. He's just waiting for that marriage to fall apart."

"What about Gatsby? He helps Gatsby's pursuit of Daisy."

"Yeah, but from the beginning, Nick knows there's something mysteriously fraudulent about him. He knows that it will eventually fall apart. That Gatsby will be a flash in the pan."

"What about Jordan Baker? Doesn't he like her? At least for a while?"

"Nick doesn't love Jordan. She's a fling. The truth of it all is Nick is a calculated romantic waiting to swoop in at the right time and save Daisy. But he knows he needs to make money first or else it won't stick."

"But she's his cousin."

Joanna waves a hand. "Distant cousin."

"But he doesn't get Daisy in the end."

"That's because it didn't work out. Things fell apart for Gatsby too quickly. Nick wasn't in a position to make a move against Tom. Since Nick's the narrator, he doesn't have to admit his defeat."

"That is an interesting theory. Do you read a lot?"

She nodded. "We should start a book club at work," she said excitedly. "Maybe we could get a few others to join us."

Us. I thought about it for a second before shaking my head. "I wish I could."

"Why can't you?"

I sighed. "I have a confession to make."

"What do you mean?"

"It's kind of embarrassing. I haven't told anyone . . . but you're going to find out anyway."

"What is it?"

"I was one of the ones who got laid off yesterday." I had been fired from the phone company, out on the street with two months' severance.

"Oh no, I'm so sorry."

"It's all my fault."

"Why would you say that? They laid off a lot of people."

"But I work—*worked*—on Y2K projects. I should have lined up something else a while ago. Like Jake did." And of course, I shouldn't have been so brazen with my boss a few months earlier. (Rebecca, my boss, had told me that it wasn't about what I had said to her, but I knew the truth. Maybe she didn't volunteer my name, but when my name did come up, I'm certain she didn't stand up to defend me.)

"Yeah, Jake told me he knew a few months ago that layoffs were coming, and anyone working on Y2K would be the first to go," she said.

"I thought they'd at least wait for us to actually hit the year 2000 before doing anything. And I thought they'd find something else for us to do."

"That's why I never took the job John offered me."

"What job?" I asked, totally surprised.

"To be his admin."

"Really?" John had never told me. This was not something that would have "slipped his mind." I was confused and annoyed by his mounting secrets.

"Yes. Then he quit like a month later, so I'm really glad I didn't take it."

"Smart of you."

"I better go find Jake," she said, grabbing my left hand and tugging slightly. "Are you coming inside?"

I couldn't resist. "Yes," I said, and we loosely held hands for a few more seconds as we walked back to the house.

My head felt like two heads, and one was slightly behind the other, like an out-of-sync voice and picture in a movie. So as we went up the steps, I took each one carefully, Joanna holding her arm around my waist.

"I'm so sorry about your head. I owe you a drink."

"I'm going to take you up on it, if only to continue that conversation about Nick and Daisy."

"Yes, please do," she said, and I took it as sincere.

We walked inside, and I told her I was going to check my head in the bathroom. She asked me if I wanted help, but I was mostly embarrassed now. I told her that I was all right.

In the bathroom, I rubbed the top of my aching head. I had a good bruise. Concussion crossed my mind—which, I thought at the time, must have meant that I didn't have one because no one with a concussion could think that straight, right?

I ruminated on my encounter with Joanna. I liked her—I was supposed to like her. She was beautiful. Smart and interesting, too. She was sweet. But her beauty was an inexplicable barrier and she stirred nothing deeper in me other than fear. The fear of inadequacy.

Chapter Nineteen

THE PARTY OUTSIDE had fallen to a simmer. It was nearly ten thirty, and, though a little skeptical, I figured the guests were being courteous to the neighbors. But then I noticed people walking about the yard with their heads down searching as if they were at an Easter egg hunt. My stomach tightened when I realized what was going on. Luda, who was carrying a drink back from the bar, confirmed my suspicions with an upward curl to her lip: "Zmeya's lost her car key."

I considered ending the whole thing and surreptitiously tossing the key on the grass near someone who was searching. But Mary came out right then and asked if she could speak with me. Her face had a determined look, as if she was ready to reprimand.

"What's wrong?" I immediately wondered if this had to do with Lauren's key.

I followed her through the dining room and into the butler's pantry. She closed the pocket doors on either side so that we were alone.

"I didn't want to make a scene earlier," she said in a hushed voice.

"A scene?"

"Upstairs when we found John with Lauren . . ."

"Come on, you don't think . . . ?" I had to play innocent, pretend that my knee-jerk reaction was to protect John.

She looked away and then rubbed her eyes. "Even though you and John are best friends, I consider you and I to have a special relationship."

I was caught a bit off guard. "Yes, me too," I said. My voice had cracked slightly, and I immediately cleared my throat.

"I think Lauren is in love with John." Her eyes fell away.

"I think Lauren is in love with Lauren," I said immediately. I didn't tell her what I suspected, that Lauren was after ruining Mary more than she was after John.

"Yes, you're right. I guess I don't mean that she's *in love* in love. What I mean is that she's in love with the idea of being married and having money and a house. I'm not saying John's done anything to reciprocate, but I don't need him to be tempted, either." She put her hand on my arm. "And you know how she is, with that hard flirty act."

"Hands down. I'd take you over her any day," I said without hesitation.

Her eyes softened. "You're so sweet." She firmly placed her hands on my cheeks and planted a kiss on my lips.

"Sorry, I'm a little . . ." She waved her arms around to indicate chaos. "I just needed to hear that."

Though I wanted nothing else but to bask in this stunned way for some time, I needed to smooth it out before it soured into an awkward silence. "Oh!" I said, maybe a bit too forced. "I have something important to tell you."

"What is it?"

"I ran into Kurt, Lauren's ex, at J. B. Flannigan's."

"I'm not surprised. He goes to Flannigan's a lot. But how do you know him?"

"I don't. He thought Lauren and I were dating."

"Dating?" she said with a scoff. "Why would he think that?"

I wasn't sure what to make of her derision: that Lauren would never date someone like me or that she knew I wouldn't date a person like Lauren. "He must have seen us talking—Lauren and I ran into each other in downtown. Is Kurt as crazy as she claims? Because he seemed normal, if not a little scared of her."

"I don't know. Lauren would tell me things he was doing, but I never witnessed any of it."

"He warned me about her—told me to look in her purse."

"Look for what?"

"I don't know. He kind of left it at that. Any idea?"

"No. None."

"Her purse is in the trunk of her car."

"How do you know?"

"Because she complained that you had stolen her perfect red purse, so she left her unperfect black purse in the trunk."

"I paid for that red purse!" Mary said indignantly. "She found it, but she didn't have any money, so I bought it. I did say if she ever paid for half, we would share it. But she never did." She shook her head.

"Why don't we find Lauren's key and look in her purse."

"How are we supposed to do that?"

"She probably dropped it when she changed upstairs. I'll bet you a hundred bucks."

"I thought you learned your lesson betting against me."

I laughed. "Yeah, I should have. If I lose, I'll give you a hundred. But if I win, you have to buy a round of mini golf."

She smiled, briefly, avoiding my gaze. We shook hands on it.

"Okay," she said. "Let's go have a look."

I followed Mary out of the butler's pantry, through the dining room and hallway, and then up the stairs. "But what could be in her purse? You sure he's not pulling your leg?"

"He might be. I don't know. He sounded pretty sincere, though. But I don't know him."

Mary walked quickly through the bedroom and around the far end and into the bathroom. The bathroom suffered the same condition as the bedroom, too large, with the double-slipper clawfoot tub and two separate vanities like islands; it was a cold room of stylish white tiles, black countertops, and marble floors.

The closet was inside the bathroom. "This is huge," I said.

"You haven't seen the closet?"

I shook my head. "No." There were gaps between hangers on the rod. "Looks like you need to do more shopping."

She laughed. "Don't tell John that."

"Now let's see where that key could be . . ."

In the middle of the room was a cabinet that had the same black countertop as the bathroom. It was there, on top, that I quietly set the key, and then pretended to be searching down on the carpet.

After a minute, Mary exclaimed, "Here it is!"

"You found it. See?"

We gave each other high fives.

"You owe me mini golf."

"Gladly," she said with a smile.

"Now let's go check out Lauren's car. Do you have a flashlight?"

"Yes, in my nightstand," she said and started for the bedroom. I followed and waited by the door as she went to her nightstand and pulled out a small flashlight.

"Perfect. Now we need a plan. We have to sneak to her car without anyone seeing us."

She removed her shoes. "These will be too loud."

I stared at her bare feet. "Her car is across the street."

"Don't worry, I'll be fine."

We decided to split up at the bottom of the stairs and meet out front. Mary would go out the front door, check to make sure no one was leaving. I would go around the back and check if anyone was coming or going through the side gate. We would meet up at Lauren's car, and if we got caught, we would simply say that we were looking for Lauren's key.

When I got outside, the noise was louder. People must have given up searching and returned to partying. When I went down the back porch steps, Lauren turned the corner.

"Have you found your key?" I said immediately.

"No. Have you seen Mary?"

"I saw her upstairs not long ago. I think she was in the bedroom looking for your key."

She stomped up the porch steps and went into the house. I took a turn around the side of the house and headed toward the front yard.

I heard my name when I reached the sidewalk. Mary was huddled near a car about thirty feet away. She pointed toward the street. I didn't see anything, but it was dark. I hunched and headed toward her. I stepped on several leaves.

Mary glared at me, and I stayed low as I finished the few steps toward her.

"Could you be any louder?" she said in a hard whisper.

"Sorry," I whispered back. "What's going on?"

"There's someone around Lauren's car."

"Who?"

"I don't know. I just ducked here."

"We don't have much time. Lauren's looking for you. I told her you were upstairs."

Someone walked up the street, and we watched to see who it was. It was hard to see through the glass of the car.

"That's John," she said.

"Maybe he was looking for her key."

"Yeah, maybe . . . once he goes into the house, let's go."

We waited there shoulder to shoulder. She looked at me and I said, "How old are we again?"

She started to giggle. She pressed her hand to her mouth to keep quiet. I kept making the shushing gesture, and that only made it worse.

As John finished crossing the street, we crept around the front of the car. There was no one else nearby. "Okay, let's go," I said.

As we walked casually to Lauren's car, Mary burst out laughing. I gave her a sidelong glance.

"Sorry," she said and made a pretend frown.

We ducked behind Lauren's car. "You'd make a terrible spy," I said.

"I know. Oh my gosh."

"Shh! Someone's coming out of the house."

"Who is it?"

"I don't know." I got back down.

Mary peeked above the car. "It's Cindy and her sister. They're going the other way."

"You have the key?"

Mary nodded. I turned on the flashlight.

"Okay, let's make this quick," I said.

I flashed the light on the keyhole. As Mary inserted the key, she said, "You have to hold the trunk. It won't stay up."

"Okay," was all I could say. We opened the trunk. This time I held on to it firmly as I pointed the flashlight inside. Mary quickly grabbed the purse.

I set the trunk down carefully, not allowing it to latch closed. Crouched behind the car, we looked inside. There was the usual—makeup, feminine products. And then Mary opened the wallet and took out a folded piece of paper. It was a sonogram. A baby. Mary stared at it. I stared at it.

"What is this?" I said reflexively.

"A sonogram. A baby."

She handed it to me.

I turned it over and at the very bottom, something in black block letters. I read out loud: "Kurt 9-6-98."

"Oh my gosh," Mary said.

I handed it back to her, and she examined it again. "I wonder if—"

Then, as if giving birth to twins, I pulled out another folded paper from the wallet and unfolded it.

"Another sonogram?" I said.

Mary took it in her hands and turned it over. She gasped. Even in the darkness, I could see she had turned white.

Chapter Twenty

"I FEEL SICK," Mary said, standing up.

I suddenly felt sick, too. Mary's face was drawn and her body shivered from her affliction. I was worried she might throw up, or worse, faint. "Take a breath, Mary." I turned off the flashlight. I wrapped my arm around her waist in case I needed to hold her up.

"I-I-I don't know how? Why?" She was gasping for air. "How, Steve?"

"Let's put these back."

I tried to take the sonogram from Mary's hand, but she held on to it firmly. Her head kept shaking. "No, no. This can't be."

I was really concerned about her, and my mind raced as I tried to think of what to do. Though at the time it felt like we were standing there for several minutes, only a half minute or so had gone by. Then, as if a switch had gone off, Mary straightened and started walking fast on the asphalt. Her steps were so hard I feared she might cut her bare feet on a piece of stray gravel. If she did, she didn't care, because there was no change in her pace.

I shoved the other sonogram into the wallet and the wallet back in the purse. I opened the trunk, threw the purse inside, closed the trunk, and took the key. By the time I started after her, she had already crossed the street.

Just as she was reaching the steps to the house, two people came out from the side gate. It was the couple who had been talking quietly in the corners of rooms and the dark edges of the yard.

Mary stopped and said something to them. That gave me the chance to catch up to her.

"Wait," I said as she started up the steps.

She stopped. "What?"

Her eyes were dark and intense, both forlorn and angry. I was afraid of her.

"What are you doing?" I said in a hard whisper.

"I'm going to confront Lauren. I mean, what is this about?" She held out the sonogram and shook it. I took it and looked at the back. "John 11-1-1999."

She looked at me evenly, while she inhaled and exhaled. "I'm fine," she said. She reached to take the sonogram back.

"I'll hold on to this. This isn't the time or place."

Her stare nearly killed me. She huffed. "Fine. But get Lauren out of here. Give her the key back. I want her out of here."

I stuck the folded picture in my back pocket. "I'm not sure she's fit to drive," I said reluctantly.

"I don't care! She has to go."

"Here," I said, handing her the flashlight. When we walked inside, John was down the hallway. "Where have you been?" he asked.

Mary didn't answer and rushed up the stairs in her bare feet.

I stood there in the entry, not sure where to go. John's face begged for an explanation.

I shrugged. "Did you ever get a fruit tart?" I asked, trying not to sound as breathless as I felt.

He shook his head. "As a matter of fact, I haven't." I followed John down the hall into the dining room. His head tilted toward the stairs. "What were you and Mary doing?"

"Mary let me borrow her flashlight. We were looking for Lauren's key."

The tray for fruit tarts was empty. As we stared incredulously, I said, "Well, there's always next year's party."

He shook his head.

"You aren't going to do this next year? A Christmas party."

Lauren barged in, glass of whiskey in hand. "John, let me borrow your car so I can get my spare key at home."

John didn't answer her.

"Can you drive?" I asked her.

"Perfectly fine." She held her arms out, and with the glass still in her hand, she started walking heel-to-toe.

I laughed. "Yeah, hold out your drink like that for the cop." I approached her and lightly bumped her waist.

"Hey! I was doing it perfectly."

John stared at me warily. Was he unhappy with me for touching Lauren or had he caught me slipping the key into her back pocket?

"I'll drive you home," I said. "Just let me have a cup of coffee first. Ten minutes." I didn't think I was in a perfect condition to drive, either, but I was in much better condition than Lauren.

I left, heading outside to the backyard for fresh air. The last hour had been too hectic, and I needed a few minutes to get myself together. My head hurt, and not just from hitting it against Lauren's trunk. It was everything that had happened. A sick feeling struck my stomach. Had I just ruined a marriage?

As I was leaning over the deck railing, I did a double take. Mary emerged from the tent, a glass of wine in her hand. How did she get there? The last time I saw her, she was heading up the stairs. And I didn't see her go down the hallway when John and I were in the dining room.

She captivated me, her bare feet on the grass, and then I gazed at her, gliding up the porch steps. She sidled up and leaned on the rail next to me.

"I gave Lauren her key back, though she doesn't know she has it," I said.

"What do you mean by that?"

"I slipped it into her back pocket."

"Without her noticing?"

I nodded. "I did it very carefully," I said, not going into details.

"I don't want her here. Why didn't you just tell her you'd found it?"

"She was drinking whiskey. I really don't think she's ready to drive. I told her that I'd take her home after I drink a cup of coffee."

"No, you don't have to do that."

"I'll drop her off at the apartment and then ditch her."

"It's fine. I'll call her a taxi," she said definitively. "I don't want you to leave."

I didn't answer. My heart was pounding hard.

She rubbed her hand up and down my back. "Thanks for being there for me."

Chapter Twenty-One

WHAT I HAD DONE WITH MARY, why I had done it, could have been easily chalked up to inebriation or maybe even a concussion. But neither of those was the reason, and I knew it. I immediately felt it in my body, how viciously wrong it had been.

What I haven't explained is what I had actually done, the part that I left out, between the first time I went to Lauren's car—when Joanna surprised me—and the time when Mary and I snuck to Lauren's car as if we were playing flashlight tag.

When Joanna startled me, I had already seen the sonogram with Kurt's name. I was putting back Lauren's purse and was lost in thought, trying to comprehend what exactly it was—a miscarriage? An abortion?—when Joanna popped out of nowhere.

That was the second sonogram I had seen that night, though the first wasn't so mysterious. Earlier in the night, I had seen Paige sharing a sonogram with the other two women on the couch.

My original plan was to give Lauren a bit of a scare. I'd take Paige's sonogram, write John's name on it, and stick it in her wallet. Whenever Lauren swapped wallets and pulled out the sonogram—days, weeks, or even months later—she'd be completely discombobulated.

So that's exactly what I did. After checking my head in the bathroom, I slipped into the adjoining bedroom where the guests had left their coats and purses. There I found Paige's purse and swiped the sonogram. I wrote John's name on it, dated it, and stuck it in my pocket.

The part with Mary was ad-libbed. I didn't plan to go to the car with her, and even then, I wasn't really planning on showing her the other sonogram. I don't know why I did it—well, I do know why. I was tired of John's act and his obscene luck.

If I had only been sober enough at that point to drive Lauren to her apartment, the story might have ended there . . .

After getting a cup of coffee (Dr. Walt's special blend might have been better), I wandered over to the side door of the garage. I was curious about what I had seen earlier. The door was unlocked, and I slipped inside, softly closed the door, and flipped on the lights.

I went back to the blue tarp where I had seen the generator earlier. I set down my coffee cup on a worktable. I lifted the tarp up completely, and next to the generator was a blue drum. I gave it a sturdy kick with my foot, and it didn't budge. Full of water, I presumed. And I was pretty sure if I looked around a little more, I'd find boxes of freeze-dried meals. On the other side of the garage in the corner I saw a safe. A gun safe? I never knew John to own guns.

As I was walking toward the safe, someone yelled, “Hey!”

Jolted, I turned around. It was John. “Geez. You scared me.”

“What are you doing?” His tone with me was unfamiliar.

“Oh, I was just walking around trying to sober up, and I ended up in here.” I don’t know why, but I felt the need to apologize. “Sorry.”

I pointed at the covered car. “Mary told me you were going to fix this. I never knew you were into cars.”

“I dabbled a little as a teenager. My next-door neighbor was always building and fixing cars. He showed me some things when I was in high school.”

“My dad, too. Except he worked on a single car since I was ten. Never finished it. Still sitting in my mom’s garage. So you’re going to fix this one?”

“Yeah, I thought I would.”

I pointed behind me. “Do you have that safe to keep guns?”

John nodded. “Yeah.”

There was a rope on a table next to me, a tangled rope, and in a nervous gesture, I picked it up and started unlooping it from one end.

“Which disaster are you preparing for?” I asked.

“All of them.”

“There are only two that I know about. And only earthquakes are real.”

He tapped the workbench with his finger. “You only know what’s happening in your own little world. But the world is interconnected. You don’t know what others are doing.”

Were we still talking about Y2K?

"True," I said, not really wanting to argue about it. I was too close to drunk and too close to concussed. My head felt swollen and was getting slightly bigger with every thump of my heart.

"Hey, you didn't tell me you almost hired Joanna to be your admin," I said, and though I was truly annoyed that he hadn't told me, it was said with a light touch.

"There are lots of things you don't know about." His tone was sharp. He turned his attention to a tool cabinet. The top was open, and he rearranged something before shutting it. He yanked on the blue tarp, which I had inadvertently left up slightly.

I could blame the alcohol or the bump on the head for what I said next, but it wouldn't be completely true. This was deliberate. "I suppose I don't know what happened between you and Lauren that night we all went out last summer."

His face suddenly turned red. "What are you talking about? You mean telling her about going into SGF to meet her that night?"

"No, not that. You looked awfully panicked after hearing Lynn's story."

"What story?" When he saw my doubtful glare, he said, "Oh, that. Come on."

"And the stroller?"

"I told you what that's all about."

"What do you think Mary thinks?" I said.

"She doesn't know anything about it," he said definitively. "There's nothing to know."

"Are you saying nothing happened between you and Lauren that one night?"

"Nothing."

"That's not what Lauren said."

"What! What did she say?"

"Basically that something happened between you two."

"No." He leaned against the workbench and crossed his arms. "No, of course not."

"So what happened?"

"Nothing. I mean, I can't really remember everything. But still . . ."

He sounded sincere.

Then he admitted that maybe something might have started to happen, loose hands in the dark, but that he tried hard not to remember it.

Could I blame him? Could I have resisted Lauren if I were drunk? Maybe not. Then again, Mary was his fiancée. "I can't believe you'd do that to Mary," I said evenly.

His face tightened. "I know you have a thing for her."

I hoped he meant Lauren and not Mary, but I wasn't certain. "Trust me. Zero feelings for her," I said forcefully. "Except maybe contempt."

"I'm talking about Mary."

"Huh?"

"I've seen you around her."

The rope in my hand was completely untangled. I tossed it on the table. "I wouldn't cheat on her, that's for sure."

"I didn't cheat on her. Don't ever bring it up again," he said angrily.

"Tell that to Mary. She already thinks you have."

His eyes widened and his nostrils flared, all of his boyish features gone. "What did you say to her?" he yelled. I had never seen him with this kind of rage. He stepped toward me and got really close. "Tell me!"

I clocked him on the face.

He fell back and grabbed his nose. "What the hell, man?"

For the briefest of seconds, I reveled in it. This was what he'd deserved since the day we were in that conference room when he was going on about the year 2000 problem.

He ran to tackle me, but I moved out of the way and threw a punch that barely made contact. We were in full fisticuffs. He threw a punch, but I moved fast, too fast, and fell hard against the car. He tried to punch me again, but I blocked and grabbed his shirt and we wrestled on the hood. He had me pinned, but then I twisted, and he slipped and fell to the ground.

"Get up!" I yelled at him. For a second I was outside myself, like someone else had taken over. I wanted it to stop.

John got up and lunged toward me, huffing, anger in his eyes. I braced myself and landed against the workbench. The porcelain coffee cup spilled and fell off the bench, crashing against the cement floor. I kicked him in the stomach with my knee. He backed up, grabbed his stomach.

As we were separated, John checked his nose, which was bleeding.

That's when we heard a loud commotion outside, and for a second we stared at each other. Did people hear us fighting and gather outside or was something else going on? John ran out holding his nose.

I stood there in the garage feeling sick and embarrassed. What had just happened was irrevocable. There could be no reconciliation. I heard more yelling. I bent down to pick up the broken pieces of the coffee cup, and that's when I realized that the sonogram was no longer in my back pocket. I looked around the floor, but it wasn't there.

I left the garage, ready to leave this party through the side yard, drive home and out of these people's lives forever. Instead, I arrived just in time to see and hear the horror unfold.

Chapter Twenty-Two

A HARD ENGINE REV. A red blur. A crunch of metal.

There was a segment of silence and stillness. Then loud screams in desperate voices.

I stood motionless, not comprehending what had just happened. My view was narrowed by the side yard gate. But there was no doubt whatever had just happened was bad. How bad? I didn't know, and for the briefest of seconds I didn't move, not wanting to know. As I ran forward, my legs got heavier, my heart pounded harder, and my vision pulsated. I was blind, I would almost say—I guess it was tunnel vision. It was only about fifteen yards, but it felt like I was running through soft, deep snow. When I did get there, I froze, shocked. What was in front of me was not immediately comprehensible.

Lauren's car was on the lawn piled up against the sycamore tree, the front of the car mangled like a wave of metal in a distorting mirror. Lauren's head was slumped against the steering wheel. A man was trying to open her door, and a woman next to him kept saying, "Oh my God!" and "Hurry!"

John was on the ground, five feet away from the tree, flat on his back on the cement. A small woman, whom I hadn't seen all night, was kneeling on the ground next to him.

I ran over and slid down onto the ground next to John. His eyes were shut and his head listed to his left. "John!" That's when I saw Mary, a body on the ground on the other side of the car. I only had a sliver of a view beneath the car, which had partially lifted up off the ground. It was too dark and my view was too blocked to see who it actually was. But I knew it was Mary. I yelled to the woman, "You got him?" But it wasn't really a question. I got up and headed around the tree.

"Mary! Mary!" Her body was twisted, her arm furled under her side. I slid down next to her. I didn't know much about giving medical attention, but I knew enough not to move her. I tried to see if she was breathing. Her face was mostly down on the ground, her body twisted awkwardly on the grass.

Joanna and Jake came toward us. "Oh my God!"

"Does she have a pulse?" Jake asked.

"I-I-I don't know. I didn't want to move her."

Joanna bent down and put her fingers on Mary's neck. "I don't feel a pulse. Can we get her on her back?"

"Yeah," Jake said, kneeling down next to her.

Where Mary's body lay, the tree had lifted the grass a bit. Jake and I moved her slowly, rolling her and getting her arm out from under her body, away from the tree and onto the flat part of the lawn. All I could think about was that this was a corpse now.

"You know CPR?" Jake asked us.

Joanna nodded. "Yes, but it's been a while." She put her hand to Mary's mouth. "I don't think she's breathing."

I looked around for bleeding but I didn't see anything.

Jake took off his jacket, folded it twice, and put it under Mary's head. "That doctor!" he said. "Is he still here?"

"I think he left," I said.

"Where does he live? Do you know?"

"I don't know," I said. I pointed. "I know he lives across the street. Over there in that direction."

"I'll find him!" he said. "I won the hundred-meter dash in high school."

It seemed a mostly irrelevant comment, but even more, one that was hard to believe given he wasn't very tall. No doubt it was true, though.

Joanna yelled, "Did someone call nine-one-one?" There was panic in her voice.

She started doing chest compressions, a couple compressions every second. What was probably twenty seconds stretched to a long while. "Where's that doctor?" I said.

Someone called out, "What's the address here?"

"Three sixteen Mistral Avenue," I yelled back.

She winced every time she pushed down.

"What can I do?"

She nodded without looking up at me. She kept on with the compressions. Then she stopped. She gasped. "Hold her head straight and tilt her head back slightly."

I moved around so I was above Mary's head. I gently moved it.

Joanna pinched Mary's nose and did mouth-to-mouth. Joanna breathed in and out twice.

She started compressions again, but when she pressed down she stopped and flicked her wrist. "Damn it!"

"Are you hurt?"

"I have a sprained wrist."

I had been watching her, and I said, "I'll do it. Just tell me if I'm doing it right." I started to push down on Mary's chest.

"Paramedics are on their way!" someone yelled.

"I hope it's more than one," I said.

"Harder," she demanded. "Harder. If you break her sternum, that's the least of our worries."

I did. Harder and faster. *Come on, Mary! Come on! You can't be dead! This can't be happening! Come on!*

A hand pushed against my shoulder. "You can stop now," Joanna said.

The edges of the scene around me came back. Slowly. As if I had gone away or fallen asleep. I had never experienced anything like that before. Lightheaded, I waited a second before standing up.

Joanna was performing mouth-to-mouth again.

Wobbly, I took a few steps around the tree to see what was happening with John. Two people were down next to him, blocking the view. Three other people, including Luda, were standing over him. Luda bent over and gave terse instructions.

"Here comes the doctor," I said, seeing Dr. Walt running down the street, barefoot, wearing sweatpants and a T-shirt, medical bag in hand. Jake was running right along next to him.

"Help!" someone yelled, a woman. They were getting Lauren out of the car, through the passenger side. I stood, not to help, but to get Dr. Walt's attention; he appeared to be heading toward them. "Mary needs help!" I yelled, and pointed down.

Dr. Walt ignored me and ran over to help Lauren.

"Get blankets!" Walt yelled. Two people, desperate to not stand around useless, ran into the house.

Joanna looked up at me. She had started the compressions again. I couldn't tell if it was a look of fear or upset or exhaustion. We needed Dr. Walt.

"Here, let me take over," I said. I got back down and did the compressions.

"We need the doctor," Joanna said, gasping.

I nodded without making eye contact and kept on with the compressions. This time my compressions weren't as vigorous. I thought we might be doing this forever, Joanna and me, going back and forth with Mary's corpse.

Joanna stopped me. She bent down to give Mary mouth-to-mouth again, but she quickly pulled back. "She's breathing! Her breath is shallow, but she's breathing."

"Yes!" Jake said. "I'll see if the doctor can come over here."

I stood up and looked over at the crowd around John.

John was sitting upright on the pavement, being held up by a man while a woman pressed a towel to his nose.

Jake returned. "He's coming now," he said. "Lauren is conscious but bleeding from her head."

We could hear sirens in the background, hope that this might all end soon.

Father Thomas, who had just come out of the house, blinked hard a couple of times. Where had he been, I wondered. I called him over, but when he saw John he ran over and knelt next to him.

Dr. Walt finally came over. Joanna explained that we had done CPR and Mary was breathing now.

"Do you know if she was hit by the car?" he asked.

"We don't know," Jake said. "But given how she was twisted, I've got to believe she was."

"Where did you learn CPR?" I asked Joanna.

She sighed, an exhausted, satisfied sigh. "I was a lifeguard in high school."

A fire truck arrived at the scene first, and as the firefighters disembarked, Dr. Walt pointed them to John and Lauren. An ambulance arrived a few minutes later, and Dr. Walt directed the paramedics to take Mary away immediately.

John had stood up, and realizing, it seemed, that Mary was not well, demanded to go with them. But he wobbled, and two firefighters helped him over to the porch and had him sit on a step.

I remained in the general vicinity, up against the tree and out of the way. I wanted to slip away, but as the paramedics took Mary on the gurney, John called out for me. I would have been more apprehensive, but he sounded more supplicating than angry. I went over to him and crouched down. He put a hand on my shoulder and asked me to stay behind and take care of the house. Apparently he didn't remember our argument or it suddenly didn't matter; I wasn't sure which.

I heard Luda say that she was going to follow the ambulance to the hospital. I asked her to call the house phone with any news. She didn't know the number and after digging out a pen from her purse, she wrote it on her palm.

A second ambulance arrived as the first one left. Dr. Walt, who had been tending to Lauren, talked to the paramedics in a hushed voice. They quickly got Lauren onto the gurney, and the ambulance left a couple of minutes later.

John was the last injured one and was being checked out by Dr. Walt, who shined a light in John's eyes. He had John follow it as he moved it back and forth. He asked John a few simple questions, and then said, "You need to be checked out for a possible concussion." A police officer standing nearby told John that he would drive him to the hospital. Father Thomas went with them.

Chapter Twenty-Three

JAKE, JOANNA, AND I SAT AT THE KITCHEN ISLAND, the house now empty except for the three of us. We sat on white upholstered stools, hunched over with our arms resting on the marble counter, each with a cup of coffee in front of us. All the lights were still on. It was as if the housewarming party had never ended, oblivious to the corrupt scene out front. Yellow tape, strung tautly, blocked off the entire yard, enclosing the ghost of trauma that had captured us and held us against our will.

I sat up and ran my hand over the counter's cold edge. We each exhaled an exhausted sigh.

"Well, this is the most exciting party I've ever been to," Jake said.

Joanna choked out a chuckle and I made a grimacing smile. Jake didn't carry any of the guilt that I did. For a second, I felt a tight camaraderie, the type that elicits unreserved openness. I reached for my back pocket, ready to pull out the stolen sonogram and explain the whole damn affair to them when I remembered that it was gone.

Mary had taken it—pickpocketed me when I was leaning over the deck railing. At least that was the only theory I could come up with.

The telephone rang.

Most people had left the house a couple of hours earlier after the police car with flashing lights quietly whisked John away to the hospital. Neighbors eased back to their houses. Guests tottering around in different states of shock—and no doubt intoxicated, too, as several taxis were called—headed home. A few helped clean up the backyard and the inside of the house, occasionally stopping to talk in adamant whispers before going back to work.

The bartender packed furiously, as if he had been serving minors and the police were looking to arrest him. He was about to toss the contents of the coffee dispenser, and I asked if he could leave it. He agreed and finished filling a box; bottles clinked as he rushed out the back gate to where his pickup truck was parked.

Dr. Walt, too, had disappeared. I thought he might have gone to the hospital in one of the ambulances, but Jake said that he had seen the doctor slip back to his house.

Every movement felt strange—as if some committee on appropriateness had to be consulted for the smallest gesture. It seemed that cleaning up lacked proper relevancy, but there was no other way to help. The SGF girls and another couple cleaned the inside of the house. Jake and I folded and stacked chairs and tables while others gathered glasses and plates.

Police were looking to take statements by eyewitnesses. They asked around, stopping anyone who was leaving, "Did you see anything that happened here tonight?" Nearly everyone denied having seen anything. When they asked me, I said that I saw nothing of the accident. "Did you observe Ms. Dalton consuming alcohol tonight?" I answered vaguely that perhaps I had seen Lauren with a glass of something at some time, though I couldn't say when or how much. I didn't mention anything about our time at Vic's.

And then all at once all the guests except Jake and Joanna were gone.

The police officer spoke to me for a minute before leaving. I asked him what he thought had happened, and he said that it appeared Lauren was turning around and hit the accelerator when she thought she was pressing the brake. And he thought alcohol was involved. I asked him about Lauren's car, mangled there on the lawn. A tow truck would be by in the morning, he said.

I was standing on the porch, watching as the officer turned off his car's flashing lights and left, when I noticed Jake in the street. It was near the spot where Lauren had been parked. Through the darkness, I couldn't really make out what he was doing. He had crouched down, and for a moment, I thought he might have been praying for Lauren. It was Mary who needed the prayer.

He came up to the house in a hurried walk. He held a coat in his arm. I was about to ask him what he had been doing when he said, "Did you see that stain where Lauren was parked?" He spoke in a hard whisper.

I shook my head. "What stain?"

Jake hung the folded coat on the porch railing. "Let me show you." I followed him down the street, which was now mostly empty of parked cars.

In the low light, there appeared to be a small puddle of liquid. I bent down and stuck my index finger in it. I rubbed between my fingers. It wasn't water. It didn't leave a dark stain like oil would have, though I couldn't be sure in the darkness. I brought it up to my nose. A fishy smell.

"Did you tell the police?" I asked Jake.

Jake shook his head. "No, I just saw it coming back from getting Joanna's coat from the car."

I never saw the police near the spot where Lauren had been parked. I don't think they suspected brake issues with her car.

"I think it's brake fluid," Jake said.

After Jake and I went inside, I told him and Joanna that I was going to wait for someone to call with news. I didn't explicitly ask John to call, but I figured he would. And though I'd asked Luda, she might not remember (or she might have washed her hands and lost the number).

Joanna said something to Jake and then asked me if they could stay a while longer and wait, too.

"Sure. Though I don't know if anyone is actually going to call," I told her.

That's when we got coffee and sat down on the stools in the kitchen.

"So what do you think happened tonight?" Joanna asked.

I told them what the officer had told me. "They'll probably charge her with drunk driving."

"Lauren was aiming her car at either John or Mary—or both. And she probably saved herself doing it," Jake said.

"What?" exclaimed Joanna. "How do you figure that?"

"She didn't get confused about what pedal to push. She wasn't *that* drunk, if she was drunk at all."

"What do you mean she saved herself?" I asked.

"Think about it. If her brake fluid was really leaking, she would have gone down that street at twenty-five miles per hour or more and hit a house or light post or whatever—or another car."

"What brake fluid leak?" Joanna asked.

Jake explained and then said, "That curb in front of the house slowed her down. She probably hit that tree at fifteen miles per hour."

"But you think she was actually trying to kill them? That's insane!" Joanna said. She frowned and incredulous lines creased her forehead.

"Scare them? Hurt them? I don't know."

The house phone rang. Joanna, Jake, and I shared glances. I got up and answered. There was only soft sobbing on the other end.

"Luda?" I said.

There was no answer, except more sobbing and catching of breath.

"Luda, what happened?"

I looked up at Jake and Joanna, who seemed to be holding their breath. I couldn't understand what Luda was saying, but

I do know my stomach dropped when I undoubtedly heard the word *dead*.

"What?" But either Luda didn't respond or I couldn't hear. I knew it was Mary. Mary had died.

I fell down to the ground, still holding the phone.

Someone else took the phone on the other side. I heard the stoic voice of Father Thomas. "Steve. I'm sorry to tell you . . . John passed."

Chapter Twenty-Four

IT WAS TWO THIRTY IN THE MORNING when I arrived home. Exhausted and unable to sleep, I sat on the couch with my feet up on the coffee table, in a dark room, unable to stare away from the blue numbers and blinking colon displaying the time on my VCR.

When Father Thomas had given the awful news about John, he'd also said that Mary was in stable condition. She hadn't been told about John's death, and it made me sick to think about her reaction. John's death wasn't real to me—that I would never see him again felt untrue. And Mary was going to feel a thousand times worse. I desperately wanted to be there for her.

After a few hours of intermittent dozing, I showered and drove to the hospital. Unsure what to do and when to do it—I didn't know if Mary had been told about John—I sat in my car and fell asleep. When I woke up it was nine thirty. I went inside the hospital and found Father Thomas in the lobby sitting area, bent over with folded hands.

"Mary's parents just arrived. They're going to tell her about John."

I sighed. "But what happened to him? He seemed fine when he left in the police car."

Father Thomas shook his head slowly. "I don't know. All I know is that he was sitting in a room waiting and when they went to check on him again, he was dead. They didn't give me any other information."

"I wonder if they're covering something up."

Father Thomas's eyes narrowed a bit. "Why would you think that?"

"Because that's what hospitals do when someone dies without explanation. They don't want to get sued." I admit that there was no basis for it, but I was upset and decidedly punchy from a lack of sleep.

"I don't know about that," he said.

"What about Mary's condition? How is she?"

"They said she was fine. Some cracked ribs, but otherwise fine."

"Any news on Lauren?"

"They released her first thing this morning."

"Have you been here all night?" I asked.

Father Thomas nodded.

"You should get something to eat," I told him, even though I hadn't eaten anything myself.

"In a bit," he said. "I wanted to wait here for Mary's parents in case they want me to talk to her or do something."

I nodded and left.

When I returned later, Father Thomas was gone. I visited the gift shop and purchased flowers before going up to see Mary. But the nursing staff wouldn't let me see her. Mary was in a critical care unit, and one of the nurses told me that a family member was with her. I dropped off the flowers with the nurse and left.

Mary called me later that day and thanked me for the flowers. "I know that you and Joanna saved me, and I'm grateful." Her voice was weak, though more upbeat than I would have figured. Maybe it was the drugs she was on, or the shock of John's death hadn't quite hit her yet.

I told her how sorry I was about John.

"I'm going to really need you over the next few weeks," she said.

Despite John's death and a wave of discomfort that regularly struck my stomach, an anxious euphoria swelled in me. "Of course," I responded evenly. "I'll always be there for you." There were plans for me to see her at the hospital the next day if she hadn't been released yet.

Between that day and the following day, when I tried contacting her, something happened. She had been moved from critical care to a general ward the day before. I couldn't get through to the general ward for an hour, and when I did they said that Mary was being released. I tried reaching her at home a few hours later, but there was no answer. Perhaps she had gone to her parents' house, but I didn't have their number. I waited for her to call me. But no call came.

The next day, after trying the house again with no luck, I called SGF, hoping to get Mary's parents' number. Luda answered. She had spoken to Mary earlier in the day. Mary was at the house and doing fine. John's funeral was set for January 5. Didn't I know? Luda asked me.

After another day passed and after leaving two messages on her answering machine, I figured she was avoiding me on purpose.

Before heading over to her house and knocking on the door, I tried Mary one more time. Though she didn't have a cell phone, John did. There was something morbid about calling that number, but I thought I'd try.

Mary picked up. I asked her how she was doing. She sounded exhausted and her answers were curt. I thought she might be mad at me because I hadn't been able to see her or talk to her. When I started complaining that she had been difficult to reach, she cut me off.

"I thought we were friends, Steve," she said.

"We are."

"Then why did you do it? Why did you trick me?"

I assumed she was talking about the sonogram. I didn't want to explain. My full explanation would have involved John and Lauren. It would have cast John in a bad light—and left me in a not much better one. Surely she would have said, "Why didn't you just tell me about it?"

I said nothing.

Mary sighed heavily. "I don't want to see you again." Then she said, "Please don't come to John's funeral."

I pleaded with her not to end it this way. She admonished me again not to attend the funeral and ended the call. That was it with Mary. She blamed me for John's death and banned me from her life.

The spiral down started after that. The shock of what had happened that night suddenly struck me as if I had been in denial. It weighed heavily on me. It was as if Mary had cursed me with replaying that night in my head over and over, my conscience inundating me with guilt. It got me low, and if I didn't take something to numb it, I started to think about ending my life.

But my survival instincts always fought back. Who actually killed John? Lauren did. She's the one who drove the car. Whether she was drunk or had bad brakes or both, she's the one who physically caused him to fall and hit his head. How about John himself? Whatever happened between him and Lauren, it was really John who started it all—I just played a small part in bringing forward his bad decisions. Could Mary be blamed? I mean, she knew that Lauren was too drunk to drive. Perhaps in her heart she wanted Lauren to hurt herself.

Then, of course, it would come back to me. I didn't intentionally want John to die, but I started the argument that caused Mary to tell Lauren to leave. This tussle went on and on, a curse à la Sisyphus or Tantalus.

Both Jake and Joanna called me after the funeral and left messages. They thought something might have happened to me. I called Jake back a week later. I picked a moment when I was sober and had the will to talk.

"All that Y2K scare and nothing happened," I said as he wished me a happy New Year.

"Yeah, I thought something, somewhere would go wrong," Jake said. "How are you? Joanna and I were worried about you."

"Honestly, not doing great. Mary blames me for John's death."

"Why? You didn't drive that car into him."

Jake didn't know that it was me who had set the events into motion. I couldn't take another person hating me, so I gave him an edited version. "If I had only driven Lauren home instead of having that cup of coffee first," I said.

"You can't blame yourself for that, man."

"Mary won't talk to me. She blames me and that's all that matters."

Jake cleared his throat. "Are you really upset because John died or because Mary won't speak to you?"

"Of course I'm upset that John died," I said.

"You're in love with Mary, aren't you?"

I don't know how he knew it. He caught me off guard, and the longer my silence went on, the more impossible it became to deny with any credibility. But I couldn't admit it out loud, either. I didn't answer him. Instead I inquired about John's funeral.

"It was a very nice service," he said. "Father Thomas told a story about John taking out cash advances on his credit cards to help him repay his college debt."

"So that he could become a priest."

"Yeah, can you believe that? I feel like I really didn't know John that well."

How did Father Thomas know about that? John had said that he didn't tell him. And then I thought maybe John had played me with his coy stories.

I launched into a bit of a rant, talking about how fortunate John had been since the very beginning. How he had been appointed on a whim to lead the Y2K conversion team. How he had lucked out with Mary, walking into SGF intending to meet Lauren and walking out with Mary's phone number. How he had made a large sum of money because he had joined the right company at the right time.

"Well, he didn't seem to be so lucky after all, did he?" Jake replied in an even tone.

It wasn't until sometime later that I learned the whole truth about John's death. John, having gone to the hospital, was seen by a doctor in the emergency room. He was diagnosed with a concussion, and as a precaution, the doctor ordered an MRI. This was at midnight. He died two hours later, having fallen asleep in a small waiting room. The hospital called it "an administrative error."

It was Jake who told me this and more, the most extraordinary part of what had happened. He called me about a month after our last conversation. He and Joanna had visited Mary at her house.

It was obvious that Mary hadn't told them what I had done, otherwise I don't think Jake would have called me. "How is she?" I asked.

"You're not going to believe this. Lauren is suing her."

"What? Lauren is suing Mary?"

"Crazy, isn't it? She's claiming that Mary knew she was in no condition to drive, and she kicked her out of the house anyway."

"Isn't Lauren being charged with anything?"

"Apparently not. A friend of her father's got her off—only has to do some community service."

Mary had told them that she was selling the house. That she couldn't live there with the memory of what had happened.

"Where is she going?"

"She's looking for a house in Campbell."

"I bet there won't be a housewarming party," I said.

"No, I'm sure not. But she did mention holding a small Christmas party."

"Really? Well, I won't be invited to that, that's for sure."

"You never know."

"She'll only invite those she likes this time."

Jake asked me what I meant by that, and I told him about the housewarming party and how Mary had invited so many people because she didn't want to exclude anyone.

"Anyway, I'm not really sure she'll be having that Christmas party," Jake said. "I think she'll have other things on her mind by then."

"What do you mean by that?"

"Mary's pregnant."

I coughed and barely got out: "What?"

"Yeah, apparently she found out just before the party. Hadn't even told John yet."

Jake said something else, but all I could think about was Mary being pregnant. I couldn't believe it. "And I haven't even told you the craziest thing . . ." That's when he told me about John, dying while waiting for an MRI. The "administrative error" turned out to be "some IT guy who decided that at midnight he was going to test a piece of Y2K code in the production system."

It wasn't something that should ever have been done. "You're kidding me, right?"

"Nope. This guy changed the clock ahead by a year. He did it for ninety seconds and then set it back. No harm, right?" Jake said sarcastically.

"So John's MRI got inadvertently moved back one year?"

"Yep. Unbelievable, right?"

"Completely," I said. "It's very ironic."

"I know. He worked on Y2K and then it killed him!"

"It's more than just that," I said. I realized this added another reason to blame John for his own death. He could have taken that job with the hospital group and fixed Y2K correctly, but instead he chose the money.

I told Jake about the job offer from the hospital to run their Y2K program.

"No way! Does Mary know about that?"

"I don't think so," I said. "They met just after that."

I asked about Joanna.

"She's doing well. By the way, she started a book club at work, and she wants you to join. She said you read a lot. I joined, but between us, I'm not sure I'm going to stick it out."

It was a kind gesture to invite me, and I didn't want to explain how awkward it would be for me. So I told him I'd think about it. "What are you all reading?" I asked.

"The Brothers Karamazov."

www.ingramcontent.com/pod-product-compliance
Lightning Source LLC
Chambersburg PA
CBHW030529310726
48979CB00010B/1852/J
9781957885001